Kevin the Brave

By
Steve Lemieux-Jordan

www.kevinthebrave.com

TABLE OF CONTENTS

FOREWORD

From the outset my intention was to write a silly version of a classic tale. The more I wrote and the more I thought about what I was writing, (every time I come back to edit I start at the beginning, not where I left off), I realized there was a lot more of me and others I have met over the years, within the tale. Furthermore I realized, like most good stories, there is a deeper imapct upon the reader below the surface story.

 I encourage you to read the surface story and accept there is a lot of silliness involved -I have been told "it's just too funny", "there are too many jokes"- and simply embrace the silliness. After doing so put the book away and in a year or two, pick it up again when your life requires you to experience a silly moment or two. What I hope happens is, suddenly you recognize a characteristic of yourself or someone close to you and the story begins to take on a whole new meaning and relevance for you.

Over the intervening years since first writing and taking the plunge into the abyss of self publishing I have reread, revised the story details but leaving the essential essence intact. If you have read earlier iterations I hope you find the changes to your liking. Many of the changes have come about from realizing my dyslexia and other, so called, learning disabilities led to some grammatical and other errors of simialr ilk. If you are a fellow dyslexic or have similar issues, the only piece of advise I can offer is persist and never let any one say you should not try taming your own dragons.

DUAL WITH A DRAGON

It was a typical sunny Saturday morning in Campaneenee, a quiet village in the foothills of the Gespachio mountain range. There were a few people hanging out in the shade of the market place, an octagonal wooden structure open on all sides with a slate roof, set, not quite, in the middle of the village square. The heavy slate roof provided some shade for the few merchants who had set up their stalls. They eagerly awaited the residents of the small village, each hoping for a good turn out on such a fine morning. A few children were playing in the dusty square, their games disturbed, occasionally, by a carriage or cart lumbering by.

A shadow drifted across the ground, one of the children looked up and shouted "Dragon!" The rest of the kids ran screaming for the shelter of the market. Unfortunately as they did, Brother Albert, of the Wiser Friends Monestry, was so startled he poured some of the monastery's famous product on a customer rather than into the large stoneware jug he was holding. The customer was not well pleased. Brother Albert, known for his convivial nature laughed and patted the nearest child on her head.

"Not to worry there's plenty more in the keg."

"I know, but now I smell like I've been bathing in beer!" Grumbled the customer.

"An improvement, then!" declared the routund friar.

"Hrrumph!, Just fill my jug." grumbled the customer.

A few adult heads looked out from the shade of the market place but the sky was as blue as it could be, with just a few fluffy clouds floating in the light breeze.

"Don't be telling fibs, trying to scare us, Cedric, or I'll tell your father!" admonished one of the adults. The children drifted back out into the sunshine and restarted their games. A few more people entered the square and headed for the market place.

Once again a shadow drifted lazily over the ground.

Once again Cedric yelled "Dragon!"

Once again the other children ran for the shelter.

Once again Brother Albert became startled and the unfortunate customer had, once again, a large quantity of Brother Albert's Succulent Sustenance poured over him. Of course most folks who enjoyed a few pints of Brother Albert's Succulent Sustenance just called it beer.

Once again heads looked out from under the shade of the market.

"That does it Cedric. When your father shows up I'm going to tell him..."

Once again the shadow drifted over the dusty ground. The adults looked skyward. A couple of them rubbed their eyes. The woman who had been admonishing Cedric, looked at him, blinked a couple of times, looked back at the now clear sky. The adults all withdrew to the shade, closely followed by the children, including Cedric. Many of the adults took a large drink of Brother Albert's beer.

No one spoke another word for almost a full minute. It had been a long time since a dragon had been seen in this part of Paassda. It had been so long that nobody believed there were any more dragons.

Suddenly there came a chorus of:

"Nah..."

"Trick of the light"

"Must have been one of those, big, green and blue dr...eagles..."

"More beer anyone?"

"Yeah, that's it..."

"Definitely not a real dragon..."

"Refill anyone?" Asked Brother Albert.

"Yeah… some kid playing with a dragon shaped kite…"

"A very big dragon shaped…"

"Very big…"

"Half price on the beer?"

For a few moments the dragon was forgotten and Brother Albert became very busy filling a wide variety of containers with half priced beer.

As this was going on a young man peered out from an upper window in the Hungry Hog Inn, which was across the street from the market place. As he did so the shadow once again drifted lazily over the square.

No one moved, except for the young man. He slowly backed away from the window as he watched the dark shape cast its even darker shadow upon the ground. A second later the young man darted from the doorway of the inn and looked up into the sky. He caught sight of a strange barbed object as it disappeared behind the rooftops across the street. He scurried back inside without saying a word.

None of the villagers noticed the young man so no one re-marked on how one moment he was not there then he was there and just as suddenly once again he was not there.

Once again the shadow returned but this time it did not drift away, it grew darker. With an earth trembling thud a huge dragon landed in the village square, her scales glinting in the bright sunlight. She flapped her leathery wings once, sending a cloud of dust billowing in all directions as she lazily folded her wings along her sides and looked around the now, seemingly, empty square.

The few villagers, who were unlucky enough to be in the square when she landed, had scattered in fear of being roasted alive. Other than the swirling dust nothing was moving, well Brother Albert was counting the money he had collected. The only sound was the deep rumble of dragon breaths and clinking coins.

A mouse ran from a corner of a building, instantly the dragon's huge yellow eyes focused on the mouse, her head snapped around as a thin stream of fire shot from her right nostril. The mouse, slightly quicker than the dragon, disappeared back into the building it had come from, brushing at its singed tail.

A strange sound began to emanate from the shadows of the Hungry Hog's doorway. The sound was like pieces of old metal slowly rubbing back and forth across each other. The dragon's ears swiveled in the direction of the sound closely followed by her huge head.

From the doorway out stepped a lone figure, clad in a suit of armor. The armor had seen better days, it did not glint in the bright sunlight. Patches of rust could be seen all over it except where the arms rubbed against the sides of the chest plate. The chest plate bore all the signs of age and abuse; it was covered in dents and deep scratches. The helmet clearly was too big for the wearer's head, for it wobbled with every step. With every step it was easy to see that the legs and shoes were less than snug. The knight had to stop and wiggle a foot back into one of the shoes. In the knight's hand a long spear, the shaft of which had clearly been repaired more than once, the point looked as dull as the suit of armor. As the knight stepped from the shadows and looked around, he had to turn the helmet with his free hand so he could see through the eye slit.

What he saw was, in the windows of every building the frightened faces of the villagers. A few cowered in the doorways of various buildings. The occupants had locked the doors and were not about to open them.

The dragon glanced contemptuously at the knight for a moment and then shifted her weight, raising her head on her long neck; she put one eye within inches of the nearest window. Purposefully ignoring the lone knight as he rattled towards her. The people inside the room of the nearest window, scrambled over each other trying to get away from the eyeball that now filled the window.

The knight crossed the square to stand directly in front of the dragon. Unfortunately he tripped over a parcel someone had dropped in their haste to find shelter. He landed with a clatter.

Instantly the dragon swung her huge head to within inches of the prone knight. She smiled, baring a glistening set of teeth that could easily crunch through an elephant. A large globule of drool slowly dripped from her lower lip splattering on dusty ground between his legs.

As the knight struggled to get back on his feet, waving away the stench of the dragon's breath, she once again reared her head to its full height and took in a lungful of air. Just as the knight got to his feet and looked up at the massive head, thirty feet above him, a fireball the size of a large carriage erupted from the dragon's mouth and hurtled to the ground.

The knight leapt to his left as the fireball hit the ground where he had been standing. The force of the resulting explosion knocked him over. He lost a shoe, exposing the hole in his sock that allowed his big toe to get some fresh air. The shoe was soon turned to a small glowing lump of molten metal. The shaft of the spear he was holding burst into flames. He dropped the burning spear and drew a small dagger from his belt.

When the dragon saw the dagger she laughed sending a series of small fireballs up over the buildings. The knight once again began to circle around the dragon looking for an opening. The dragon's tree trunk like legs stumped around trying to keep the knight in front of her. As she swung her massive body her tail followed and knocked the roof from the market place. A few screams from within soon turned to moans as most had spilled the last of Brother Albert's Succulent Sustenance over each other.

The knight knew he had to stop the dragon before she could do any more damage to the village or its residents. He feinted to the right and ran at the dragon, she reared her head, sucking in another lungful of air. Again she blew a massive fireball at the knight. The fireball descended, engulfing the knight who had suddenly stopped moving.

The villagers could not believe their eyes, more so they could not believe they now would be the victims of the dragon's pleasure.

The fireball lifted and faded into the sky. All that was left of the knight was a rusty suit of armor glowing a bright shade of orange.

Some of the more sensitive villagers turned away from the sight. Others watched in disbelief as a small dagger spun through the air, sparkling as the sunlight caught the blade. The dagger hit its target with surprising force and accuracy, the tip slipping in between the edges of two steel hard scales.

The dragon had been stumping around the village square in victory; suddenly she stopped and tried to look at the tiny dagger poking from her chest. With a roar that rattled the windows, she leapt into the air howling as she few off.

The little dagger had pierced the one spot in a dragon's scales that causes so much pain they fly off trying to get away from the stinging blade. More often than not the dagger or whatever falls out after a few miles causing no lasting physical harm. There was one time when a dagger had fallen out and landed on a very warty toad.

No one dared move or make a sound, unsure of the dragon's demise. Then a lone figure strode from the shadow of a nearby shop front, dressed only in his underwear. It was then the onlookers noticed the back of the still glowing armor was hinged and swinging in the breeze.

The cheer from the villagers equaled the roar from the dragon, rattling windows near and far. A few began chanting. As the chant swelled and became coordinated the knight smiled, as his name echoed off the buildings surrounding the square.

"Kevin, Kevin, Kevin, Kevin The Brave." over and over, louder and louder..

ABOUT KEVIN AND WHERE HE LIVED.

Kevin-the-Brave was not always called Kevin-the-brave. His name was just plain Kevin. Well, to be absolutely correct, his name was not "Just Plain Kevin," his name was just Kevin.

That doesn't sound right either. What I mean is the people who knew him would have said things like:

"Look, there goes that kid Kevin."

They would *not* have said things like:
"Look, there goes that kid, Just Kevin."
"Just Kevin? Don't you mean Just Plain Kevin?"
"No, I mean Just Kevin. Who on earth, is Just Plain Kevin?"
Of course, they might have said something like:
"Oh, that's just Kevin, going to school."
Unfortunately Kevin's last name just happened to be Plane, so technically his name was Kevin Plane. Therefore you might have heard people saying things like:
"There goes that Plane kid, Kevin", or
"Oh, that's just Plane, Kevin, going to school."
All that aside, it did not help that Kevin was not particularly handsome nor was he overly ugly, he wasn't really tall or short, super clever or terribly dumb. He was to all intents and purposes mostly rather ordinary; some would say Kevin was just… well…plain.
Mostly.
More about that later.
Kevin lived with his parents, who owned an inn called "The Big Bore". The name was supposed to be "The Big Boar" as in large

male pig but the local sign maker, Dizwald Lexia, while very good at painting was terrible at spelling. "The Big Bore" was in a village called Lassaggnee.

The village of Lassaggnee was in the Kingdom of Blognasee, which was in the land of Paassda. The part of Paassda that was Blognasee was very pleasant, full of rolling hills, green fields, a large forest, a few small woods, some streams, and a river that meandered through the land and the center of Lassaggnee.

The land around Lassaggnee was mainly used for farming and as there was no heavy industry polluting the atmosphere, the air was nice and clean. Another reason for the air being nice and clean was the internal combustion engine had not been invented yet.

Most Blognassians got where they were going by walking or riding on horses or other large animals. The farmers, and the more well to do people, had some sort of cart or fancy carriage that could be pulled by horses or other large animals.

Those Blognassians, who did not have horses or other large animals, carts or fancy carriages, complained the most about all the ...um... "...pollution..." left behind by the horses and other large animals. This was not unreasonable, as they, the horses and other large animals, tended to ...er... relieve themselves whenever and wherever they wanted. The downside was one had to be very careful where one walked. The upside was that there was plenty of natural fertilizer for growing wonderful roses.

If there was an industry in Blognasee, it was the rose industry. The roses were mostly used for decoration but many varieties were grown for medicinal purposes, making tea, perfume, or even wine and beer. There were rumors that more than a few rose varieties had special, if not magical, properties. However, the vast majority of Blognassians did not believe those rumors.

One person who did believe in the magical properties of roses, Hyacinth McThornbush, wrote a beautifully illustrated book called "The Magical Properties of Roses." Her book listed all the names, both scientific and colloquial, the type of soil each variety thrived in and the best time of year to plant particular roses. The book also carefully cataloged all of the "magical" qualities of certain strains, where to find, and even when to pick them to maximize their "magical" might.

A few weeks after her book was published it was discovered Ms. McThornbush's accounts of the magical properties of roses, were not based on any scientific facts backed up by years of extensive research. Hyacinth's book, it was revealed, turned out to be just a collection of recounted old wives' tales she had heard as she traveled about Paassda.

Along with the old wives' tales was a lot of text copied from brochures she had collected from some of the big rose farms. Even the beautiful illustrations were copied from the very same brochures. As a result, her book was not particularly popular and did nothing to change the opinions of those who did not believe in the magical properties of roses. Consequently the book did not sell very many copies. Ironically, that makes the book all the more desirable and valuable now, just ask your nearest bibliophile.

There were a few other villages scattered around the kingdom of Blognasee, the biggest though, was Lassaggnee. Lassaggnee nestled in the middle of a quiet valley and was on the main road that rambled its way through Blognasee, where it crossed the Reecotta River.

By today's standards, Lassaggnee was quite small and very quaint. The main road ran through the middle of the village. Unfortunately the road was not quite wide enough for even the narrowest of carriages to pass each other. This led to terrible traffic jams as getting a pair of horses or other large animals, to back up was difficult at the best of times, let alone while they were trying to pull a cart or carriage. It was not made any easier with all sorts of people yelling instructions to the drivers and or the horses or other large animals.

The buildings on either side of the main road were all made of rough hewn timbers and coarse plaster with thatched roofs.

Lassaggnee did not have any shopping malls or huge department stores. There was a market place, where traveling merchants could set up in the center of the village and sell their wares. Around the market place were a few shops, a grocer, a butcher, a baker, and a candlestick maker.

On the outskirts of Lassaggnee, there was a small schoolhouse, an inn ("The Big Bore"), a couple of bed-and-breakfast places and Rusty-the-blacksmith's smithy.

The total population of Lassaggnee, for any statisticians who happen to be reading or listening to this story, was approximately 357.

A short distance from Lassaggnee, across the Reecotta River, was a castle. King Archibald the XXVIII (28) lived in the castle with his queen, Hortense, and their daughter Princess Maybel.

King Archibald was generally considered to be a good king unless you upset him. The easiest way to upset King Archibald was to call him "Archie". The mere act of calling King Archibald, "Archie", would result in instantaneous banishment to the deepest dungeon in his castle. There were other ways to upset King Archibald but it will take too long to explain all of them here.

King Archibald's castle was not the biggest castle in the world, but the people who lived in and around this particular castle did not travel very far, so it was the biggest they had ever seen.

The castle was built on top of a flat-topped hill, which is about the best place for a castle. If you were to travel more than a couple of miles away you could still see it quite clearly, and anybody in the tallest tower could see you. That is, if the person in the tallest tower happened to be looking in your direction, and you were not hiding behind a tree, or something else.

The tallest tower was indeed very tall and was called "The Tall Tower." The rest of the castle was like most castles.

If you want, and already know all about castles, you can skip the next couple of paragraphs, but for those of you who are less informed, about castles that is, read on.

The castle had four massive walls that made up an irregular rectangle. At each corner of the rectangle was a round tower that was a few feet taller than the walls. More or less in the middle of the front wall, on either side of an entryway, were two smaller towers. All the towers had narrow windows that were used for shooting arrows at an attacking army. On top of all the towers and walls were crenellations or big notches. From there, the people in the castle could throw all sorts of stuff down onto an attacking army and then hide from the arrows of the attacking army behind the upright parts. The towers also housed the people who lived and worked in the castle. Built onto the back wall of the castle was the keep, this was the main residence for the king and his family.

A pair of heavy wooden doors and a portcullis protected the main entrance to the castle. A portcullis, if you do not already know, is a very heavy gate like thing that drops down to stop an attacking army from getting into the courtyard. There was also a drawbridge, which could be raised to cover the gateway and portcullis. When the drawbridge was down it bridged a moat that surrounded the castle. Again, for those of you who are unfamiliar with the various parts of a castle, a moat is a deep ditch around the outside of a castle and is normally filled with water. This particular moat was not filled with water. It did have some water, maybe a foot at most, but largely it was filled with weeds and the rubbish and other …stuff… the people who lived in the castle had thrown out of the narrow windows, or from the crenellations, not necessarily at an attacking army. As a result the last thing anyone wanted to do was fall into the moat. Moats are also meant to keep an attacking army from getting into the castle. As you have probably gathered by now, castles were built for people who were more than a little concerned about being attacked by an army, or anything else for that matter.

Here would be a good place to start again, if you had decided not to read the details about the castle.

Among the other residents of the castle were; a couple of other royal family members, a few people who helped run the kingdom, some servants, a whole bunch of soldiers, a heck of a lot of horses and about thirty-eight crows.

The soldiers who lived in the castle were known as the King's Guard. In most kingdoms only the best soldiers become guardsmen, but as these were the only soldiers in this particular kingdom, it didn't really make much difference whether they were good or not. As long as you were willing to do battle with an attacking army, fight off a dreadful monster, or even rescue the odd damsel in distress, you could become a member of the King's Guard.

Being a member of the King's Guard was also the best job a young man (young women were not expected to do that sort of thing in those days) could get. After all, there was the potential of adventure, travel to foreign lands, plus you got free clothing, free food, lodgings, and you were paid. You were not paid a lot but it was better than a slap-in-the-face-with-a-wet-fish.

By the way, in case you are wondering, being slapped-in-the-face-with-a-wet-fish used to be one of the more popular forms of punishment back then. Another, not so popular, punishment was a good old fashioned, poke-in-the-eye-with-a-sharp-stick.

As I mentioned earlier, there was a very tall tower built into the back wall of the castle opposite the main gateway. The Tall Tower looked a bit like a very tall lighthouse jutting out of the roof of the keep.

The entrance to the keep was atop a wide and grandiose staircase that swept up to a huge ornate doorway. The huge ornate doorway led to the Royal Apartments. Off to one side, away from the wide and grandiose staircase and huge ornate doorway, was a much smaller and very drab doorway leading to a very narrow staircase. The very narrow staircase twisted its way up to the top of the Tall Tower and nowhere else.

A few miles from the castle, there was a long mountain range, the Gespachio mountains. The foothills of the mountains were covered by a very large and very dark forest. The forest was regarded by most people as a very scary place and almost no one went there. The Blognassians had named the forest, "The Dark and Scary Forest." Along with the forest being very dark and very scary, there were all sorts of tales about all sorts of monsters that inhabited the "Dark and Scary Forest".

According to another local legend, one area of the mountain range, near the Dark and Scary Forest, was where the local dragon lived. No one had actually seen a dragon for a long, long time, there again, anybody who ventured near the place where the dragon was rumored to live, was never seen again either. An even longer time ago, some people built a village on the edge of the forest, near where the dragon was rumored to live but they all disappeared, and the village was never re-inhabited.

Among all the other rumors about the Dragon of Blognasee, was one telling of the time, many centuries ago, when the dragon had stolen most, if not all, of the treasure in the kingdom. This may have something to do with why King Archibald was regarded by the kings from the surrounding kingdoms as more of a "poor cousin" than a peer. Anyway, it was all just a bunch of rumors which none of the sensible locals believed.

Most of the people in and around Lassaggnee knew Kevin, but did not devote a great deal of thought to him. If the villagers did think about Kevin, they usually sighed, made tut-tut sounds, shrugged their shoulders, or tried to change the subject.

The reason they did not want to talk about Kevin was because most had rather painful memories of Kevin and his uncanny ability to cause havoc wherever he went. This was due, in part, because the other kids who lived in and around Lassaggnee enjoyed nothing more than teasing Kevin and chasing him all over the place. Unfortunately, for Kevin, he was easily scared by pretty much anything. Loud noises, small animals, dark spaces, high places, large animals, the list goes on. Every time he heard a loud noise, came across a small or large animal, went into to a dark or high place, he would turn and run.

All that running away was great exercise and eventually Kevin learned to run very fast. Kevin ran so fast that if the other kids said "Boo", he would be on the other side of the village almost before you could say his name.

When Kevin ran fast he would frequently knock someone or something over as he careened around a corner. More often than not, he would run straight into the fruit and vegetable racks of Grean-the-Grocer, scattering fresh fruit and vegetables all over the street. The scattered fruits and vegetables were shortly thereafter trampled into the muddy street by at least twenty-three pairs of youthful feet as the other kids tried to catch Kevin.

The villagers became quite accustomed to Kevin racing around the village, and could tell, roughly, what time of day it was by just taking note of the direction in which Kevin was running. Knowing when Kevin and the other kids would be racing around the village was very useful to Grean-the-grocer. It gave Grean-the-Grocer time to put up wooden barriers to deflect Kevin away from his racks of fruits and vegetables. Mind you, it did take Kevin a couple of months before he stopped running into the barriers. He then moved on to just glancing off them, and eventually to missing them altogether.

Incidentally, Kevin's father had invented the barriers. He had become so exasperated with Grean-the-Grocer banging on his door complaining about all the fruits and vegetables that had to be thrown out because they had been trampled into the muddy street, by at least twenty-three pairs of youthful feet. Each time it happened.

"Who's going to pay for all these fruits and vegetables that have been trampled into the ground because your son knocked them over?" Grean-the-Grocer would demand.

Kevin's father, Barry (also known as Bar-the-Bar because he usually worked behind the bar), would grumble and pay Grean-the-Grocer.

Grean-the-Grocer, though, did not mention, to Bar-the-Bar, that he was selling the mashed fruits and vegetables to a pig farmer, Melvin Beaff. Melvin was also known as Mel-the-Smell, if you want to know why he was called Mel-the-Smell visit a pig farm someday. Mel-the-Smell's farm was a couple of miles outside the village. Mel-the-Smell was very pleased with the growth of his fertilizer business.

Mel-the-Smell's fertilizer business had grown because his customers were very pleased with the quality of the fertilizer, which helped them win all sorts of prizes for their roses. A fact he bragged about whenever he had a few pints of ale in Barry's inn. In return, Bar-the-bar did not let on to Grean-the-Grocer that he was charging Grean-the-Grocer a few extra schillinks each time he came into the inn for a meal or a drink.

Schillinks, by the way, were the highest valued coin in Blognasee. Each schillink was made up of thirteen pentsos and each pentso was made up of twenty-one qgtdgts. But as no one knew how to pronounce qgtdgts, and their "street" value was virtually non-existent, because everything cost at least one pentso, none of the Blognassians bothered with qgtdgts. Well, a few numismatists (coin collectors) did, but this story is not about them. However, it is worth noting that qgtdgt coins, due to their rarity, were worth several schillinks to the more avid numismatists.

As Kevin grew older, his habit of running from anything remotely scary did not change, much, but he did become quite useful to the villagers. When he ran past, they would often give him a package or a letter to deliver to someone's farm or shop or house.

There was only one time that Blough-the-Glassmaker gave Kevin a package. The cuts Kevin sustained were nothing compared to those suffered by Di-the-Widow when Kevin crashed into her with Blough-the-glassmaker's package, but nobody was seriously hurt.

In fact, it was very rare for anyone to get seriously hurt in Blognasee. Some claimed it was due to the rose-wine and rose-beer everybody drank; others said it was due to an evil spell cast by a wicked witch. Of course, that theory was not taken very seriously, mostly because there are very few wicked witches who cast evil spells, which turn out to be anything but evil. Most of the wicked-witch-theory people also believed in the magical powers of the roses. The wicked-witch-theory did not help their cause or gain them any more respect.

The kids chasing Kevin would not take any parcels, as Cirloin-the-butcher found out. Poor Cirloin-the-Butcher had to stand by and watch as twenty-three pairs of youthful feet gleefully trampled a fine cut of pork into the muddy street.

Kevin's father, as I said earlier, owned the "The Big Bore Inn." Barry had tried to forgive Diz-the-Paint, the sign painter, for misspelling the name of the tavern. After all, Dizwald had painted a very lifelike picture of the large pig before he painted the words above it.

Luckily for Barry, most of the other villagers did not know that the correct way to spell the word for a male pig is B-O-A-R not B-O-R-E. For a long time Barry had to put up with some, mostly, good-natured jokes from the few customers who did know how to spell. After a while Barry grew used to the jokes and just smiled pleasantly as he took their money. Eventually, only the occasional merchant, especially ones who had not visited Lassaggnee before, bothered making jokes. However, as everyone else had already heard every boring joke, they did not even smile.

Barry was not the only one upset with Diz-the-Paint. One of the others was Grean-the-Grocer. Grean-the-Grocer was displeased because the sign above his door read "Grean'z Gropery Shoppe". He was not entirely unhappy though as the mouth-watering painting of succulent fruits and vegetables attracted more customers than before the sign went up.

Cirloin-the-Butcher was not very happy with his sign either, "Sirlion's Botchery" but as he was now busier than ever, serving customers who swore they could detect the aroma of roast beef every time they looked at his sign, Cirloin-the-butcher was not very unhappy either.

Kevin's mother, Martha, who was always the more forgiving of his parents, simply said they should be grateful as no doubt "...those in the know..." would recognize the skills of Diz' Slexia and someday name a style of painting after him.

"Therefore..." she tried to convince Barry, "...the painting of the pig will be very valuable."

Barry was not convinced and had long since given up trying to explain it was not the picture he found at fault. Grean-the-Grocer and Cirloin-the-Butcher were unconvinced too. For the record, Diz-the-Paint thought the signs were perfect and refused to repaint them.

After school, when he had finished running about the village, Kevin helped his parents at the inn, serving the soldiers and other patrons their libations. Unfortunately, Kevin was not a well-coordinated person so it was not unusual for several patrons to find themselves drenched in rose-beer because Kevin had tripped over someone's foot, or a stool, or the occasional drunk who had collapsed onto the floor.

Whenever Kevin could he would sit with the old soldiers. He loved to listen to the stories they told, about fighting battles, slaying dreadful monsters, or rescuing the odd damsel in distress here and there. Not that the distressed damsels were particularly peculiar, it is really a question of frequency or the lack thereof.

One thing worth noting here is the adventures the soldiers told of usually became increasingly hazardous, and their deeds greater and braver as the evening wore on. This may have had something to do with the effect of consuming large quantities of rose-beer or rose-wine or other libations.

Kevin did not realize most of the soldiers could not remember the last time they had to do any *real* battle fighting, dreadful monster slaying, or even distressed damsel rescuing.

Now if you remember, I said earlier Kevin would run from almost anything, while true, Kevin did like to daydream that, he too could go off with the guardsmen fighting battles, slaying dreadful monsters, or even rescuing the odd damsel in distress here and there. So he was brave at heart.

KEVIN GETS A JOB.

When Kevin reached the age, we all reach, and it became time for him to find a job, other than helping his parents at the "Big Bore Inn", he immediately applied for the King's Guard, to everyone's amazement, he was accepted into their ranks.

It was, after all, the least they could do, as many of the soldiers had made small fortunes thanks to Kevin. The soldiers would often make bets with the merchants who passed through the kingdom and stayed at The Big Bore Inn. The bets, more often than not, involved a certain boy, and when he would careen through the inn covered in bits of vegetables, or who would be next to have a tray of overflowing beer glasses tipped over them. They never lost. Well, almost never. A young Lieutenant, whom nobody liked very much, made a bet with a merchant who had stayed at the inn before.

The merchant was able to persuade the Lieutenant to wager on the actual vegetables that would adorn Kevin as he crashed through the bar. What the merchant did not tell the Lieutenant was he, the merchant, had just sold Grean-the-Grocer some unusual vegetables, which were only grown in a far-off part of Paassda. That night the merchants celebrated long and heartily at the expense of the young Lieutenant.

Soon after Kevin was enlisted, it started to dawn on the villagers just why the Captain-of-the-Guard had accepted Kevin as a guardsman, apart from all the gambling.

Kevin was the perfect messenger.

Or so the Captain-of-the-Guard thought.

Kevin was, without doubt, extremely proficient at running

about the village and knew every nook and cranny, every stone, and every rut left by every cart. He could also run very fast, faster than most of the horses. The trouble was it would take days for him to run a message to the next village, which was, at most, a day's quiet stroll from the castle. Not because he was too slow but because he would run so fast that he would run through the village before he realized, and end up miles away. Then when he turned around and ran back, he would run right past the village again because he was in such a hurry. Every now and then, he would miss the turning for the right road and get lost in the lanes leading to the various farms. It was a little like watching the ball in a pinball machine bouncing around.

When the intended recipient of the message was able to catch Kevin it often turned out that Kevin had forgotten what the message was, or had left it behind.

Then there was the day that Kevin was running toward the village of Poot-a-Neska, when a field mouse inadvertently ran across the road in front of Kevin. Kevin was not good with animals large or small, in fact most animals scared him, which is why he ran as fast as he could back to the castle and dove under his bunk (his fear of dark places was nothing compared to his fear of animals) before anyone could stop him.

To be honest he had run so fast that no one saw him. The only reason they found him was the bunk, he was trying to hide under, was home to a small family of house mice. When one of them ran over his foot Kevin jumped up, tipping the bunk over onto the next one and that bumped the next one. The sound of bunks crashing into one another brought all the soldiers running into the barrack room. It took Kevin a couple of days to put everything back in place.

About a month after the incident with the field mouse, and Kevin had taken two weeks and several attempts to deliver another message to the village of Spag-Bol, near the Dark and Scary Forest, the Captain-of-the-Guard made a decision. He decided maybe Kevin was not cut out to be a messenger after all. The Captain-of-the-Guard told his Lieutenant to tell the Sergeant-at-Arms to start training Kevin as a combat soldier.

A week later, the Captain-of-the-Guard made another decision. The new decision was prompted by several of his best instructors being wounded by Kevin's total ineptitude, with a sword or any other weapon. At one point Kevin had come very close to cutting his own ear off while trying to put his sword back in its scabbard. I was told he had tried putting the sword in hilt first.

It all came to a head when the Captain-of-the-Guard stepped out of his quarters to get some fresh air. The Captain-of-the-Guard stood on a small landing at the top a short flight of wooden steps that led to his door. He looked around and saw Kevin trying to master the art of archery. Kevin, standing about twenty-two feet away from the Captain-of-the-Guard, facing the targets (they are actually called butts, but I don't want you kids to start giggling uncontrollably thinking about people shooting arrows at their hindquarters, even though Kevin had managed to do just that at least once) the targets were propped up against the far wall of the castle.

The Captain-of-the-Guard was just beginning to wonder why the lone instructor was crouched down behind Kevin's knees, and where everybody else was, when an arrow hissed past his face, close enough for him to feel the feathers brush the tip of his nose. Kevin spun around, and fell over the instructor as he tried to see where the errant arrow had gone. When he and the instructor had finished falling over each other as they tried to stand up again, Kevin looked up and saw the arrow still quivering in the door of the Captain-of-the-Guard's office.

The Captain-of-the-Guard, as white as a sheet, was glaring furiously at Kevin. Kevin took a moment or two before he decided it was probably better to leave the arrow where it was, and return to the barracks. The longbow Kevin had been using barely touched the ground before the door of the barracks, on the other side of the courtyard, slammed shut behind him. The lone instructor, who had once again crouched down protecting his head with his arms, slowly uncovered his head and looked around. After making doubly certain that Kevin was no longer in the courtyard, he stood up and strolled back to the barracks.

As Kevin sat on his bunk he began feeling a little sad and as though he could get nothing right, no matter how hard he tried. The rest of the soldiers mostly ignored him or when they did look at him they would slowly shake their head. This did not help Kevin's mood. He spent the rest of the evening curled up in a ball feeling sadder and sadder.

That evening the Captain-of-the-Guard, the Lieutenant, and the Sergeant-at-Arms sat down and discussed what they were going to do with Kevin.

Early the next morning, the Captain-of-the-Guard, once again standing outside his office, told the Sergeant-at-Arms to bring Kevin to him. The rest of the soldiers were busy practicing combat drills and so on in the castle's courtyard. There was a lot of noise. Kevin was trying on some armor outside the barrack room. He was not being very successful.

When the Sergeant-at-Arms tapped Kevin's shoulder, to tell him that the Captain-of-the-Guard wanted to see him right away, Kevin jumped up, sending bits of armor flying off in many directions. One piece (I think it was a foot) flew into a horse-trough, startling the horse drinking from it. The horse reared up, tipping its rider off, sending him crashing into a group of archers who had just loaded their longbows with arrows. The arrows were spontaneously released into the air. The arrows, equally spontaneously, returned to earth barely missing the men from the local brewery on the other side of the courtyard. The men from the local brewery were unloading half a dozen large kegs of rose-beer into the soldiers' mess hall (that's the room where the soldiers eat when in the castle, and it is usually quite tidy, so I have no idea why it's called a mess hall). The beer kegs rolled off the cart all by themselves because the men from the brewery were now pinned to the ground by a dozen or so arrows that had missed injuring them, but had managed to pierce their shoes, pinning them to the ground. Probably one of the few times those fashionable long-toed shoes were greatly appreciated by their owners, or maybe not, depending how you looked at the situation. This may be why that particular style of shoe is no longer considered fashionable.

One by one, the huge kegs rolled across the courtyard, all the while gathering speed, due to the slope of the courtyard, and crashed into the castle wall, whereupon they burst, sending a thick foamy shower of rose-scented beer over the royal laundry that had only a few minutes before been hung out to dry.

Meanwhile Kevin was sprinting across the courtyard; as he did, anyone within ten feet of his path moved as quickly and as far away as possible. The Sergeant-at-Arms did not follow Kevin; he could only turn slowly around, his mouth agape, and stare at the chaos that only a few moments ago was unthinkable. Kevin skidded to a halt in front of the Captain-of-the-Guard, who was waiting outside the door to his quarters, and saluted smartly. Well, as smartly as anyone with the leg from a suit of armor encasing his arm could.

The Captain-of-the-Guard did not return the salute as he was staring at the trail of turmoil Kevin had created. He slowly turned his attention to Kevin who was still saluting, partly because the Captain-of-the-Guard had not returned the salute, and partly because Kevin could not get his arm down again, the knee joint of the armor had locked up.

When the Captain-of-the-Guard, after, eventually, returning Kevin's salute several times, realized Kevin could not move his arm, he ordered a pair of soldiers to help remove the armor. The soldiers were reluctant to get anywhere near Kevin, but as the penalty for disobeying an order was twelve slaps-in-the-face-with-a-wet-fish they did as ordered.

They could have opted for the alternate penalty of six-pokes-in-the-eye-with-a-sharp-stick, but that meant they would not be able to see for several weeks and would lose their pay, as they would not be able to do their duties. It was indeed a very rare occasion that anyone went for the pokes-in-the-eye-with-a-sharp-stick option. A few of the old soldiers, who had gone for the poke-in-the-eye-with-a-sharp-stick option, were still around and enjoyed scaring kids with their bad eye. Mostly they sat at the bar of the Big Bore Inn offering sage advice, to those who bought them a drink, on how to avoid the Sergeant-of-the-sticks. It was the Sergeant-of-the-sticks job to make sure that there was always a plentiful supply of sharp sticks, and to carry out any poking-in-the-eye-with-a-sharp-stick punishments.

It took the two soldiers a few minutes to extract Kevin from the offending leg of armor. As Kevin was being extricated from the armor, the Captain-of-the-Guard tried very hard to ignore the commotion that was going on behind Kevin. All the other people in the courtyard were trying to clean up the mess Kevin had inadvertently created.

"Plane, Kevin, I have decided you should be promoted." The Captain-of-the-Guard said raising his voice above the surrounding clamor.

Those closest to the Captain-of-the-Guard stopped what he or she was doing and turned to whoever was behind them and told them to stop what he or she was doing. Soon, like a ripple in a pond, people were stopping whatever it was they were doing and turning to see what was going to happen next. The ripple effect reached the village and beyond. Even the horses in the stables stopped munching their oats. There was not a single sound in the castle courtyard. It was so quite you could have heard a pin drop.

As it happens somebody did drop a pin, but it fell onto the grass, so no one heard it. Nevertheless, they would have, if it had dropped onto a stone or something hard. What they did hear, was the person who dropped the pin say,

"Oh bother! I've dropped a pin."

Several others then said, "SHUSH!"

The Captain-of-the-Guard looked past Kevin momentarily, and saw a huge crowd quietly gathering behind Kevin. Everyone in the crowd was looking at the Captain-of-the-Guard as though he had just gone stark raving bonkers. The Captain-of-the-Guard cleared his throat and returned his gaze to Kevin. A small smile played on the Captain-of-the-Guard's lips. The smile suddenly stopped. The Captain-of-the-Guard frowned upon such behavior.

Kevin was beaming up at the Captain-of-the-Guard. Kevin, as I have already mentioned, was not too bright. Some of the more mean spirited villagers, like Ms. Flower-the-baker, had said that Kevin was a few slices short of a loaf. Others, like Mr. Wackz-the-candlemaker said that if Kevin were a candle, there would be no wick. Grean-the-grocer often said that Kevin was just a few grapes shy of a bunch.

Surprised, Kevin was not sure how to react to the news of his impending promotion, he snapped to attention and saluted again, this time knocking his helmet off. As Kevin scrambled to pick up his helmet, the Captain-of-the-Guard rolled his eyes in the most exasperated fashion you could think of, and frowned again. The Captain-of-the-Guard, while rolling his eyes, thought it would be nice if the soldiers' uniforms actually fit them.

"Why is it, the Chancellor keeps insisting the quartermaster order from the worst uniform makers?" the Captain-of-the-Guard mused, for what felt like the ten billionth time. He then tried adjusting his own ill-fitting uniform. (The quartermaster is the one responsible for obtaining all the supplies for the soldiers). Curiously, though, both the quartermaster and the Chancellor always seemed to be well dressed.

When Kevin had recovered his helmet, the Captain-of-the-Guard beckoned Kevin to ascend the steps and join him on the landing. Kevin did as ordered, stamped to attention and once more, he began to salute. The crowd ducked instinctively. Quick as a flash the Captain-of-the-Guard grabbed Kevin's arm.

"At ease soldier" the Captain-of-the-Guard ordered.

Kevin stood at ease. The Captain-of-the-Guard breathed a sigh of relief.

So did the crowd.

"Plane, I have decided you shall be promoted to the highest position in the King's Guard."

The crowd gasped. Quietly, but still the crowd gasped, the Captain-of-the-Guard heard. As he frowned upon gasping as well as smiling, he frowned at the crowd.

"Why? Is the Captain-of-the-Guard retiring?" someone whispered.

"More to the point, why would he give Kevin his job?" Someone else asked.

"Shush!" said the rest of the crowd.

Kevin had overheard and was bursting with pride.

"I'm going to be the new Captain-of-the-Guard." Kevin thought excitedly.

The Captain-of-the-Guard rolled his eyes again. Kevin was thinking the Captain-of-the-Guard rolled his eyes a lot, almost as much as he frowned.

"Plane, you will this day be given the safe... er... tall... um... most prestigious position available..."

"Er... Excuse me Captain, you said the highest..." Kevin interrupted, which shocked everybody, as they all thought Kevin would not dare to say boo to a mouse, especially a field mouse. Kevin was so thoroughly excited about his promotion he wanted to make sure he got everything he deserved.

The crowd gasped again.

The Captain-of-the-Guard glared at Kevin for interrupting, yet another behavior he frowned upon. He then glared at the crowd for gasping again. A few of the people were giggling and as the Captain-of-the-Guard frowned upon that behavior as well, he (yep, you guessed it) frowned even more. The Captain-of-the-Guard was frowning so hard he was having difficulty not frowning.

At this point, the crowd included most of the villagers, and even more people were streaming into the courtyard. Rumors of the Captain-of-the-Guard's failing sanity and or Kevin's impending promotion had spread throughout the village and beyond. It did not matter who heard which rumor, the interest generated was so compelling that whoever heard, immediately stopped doing whatever it was they were doing, and headed straight for the castle.

"...Your new position carries great responsibilities and requires you to be on duty twenty-four hours a day. You will be obliged to keep a constant vigil from the highest …," The Captain-of-the-Guard continued trying to ignore the curious stares from the crowd.

One of the older soldiers, in the crowd, rolled his un-poked-in-the-eye-with-a-sharp-stick, eye skyward. He then whispered something to his friend who did the same thing with his un-poked-in-the-eye-with-a-sharp-stick eye, and smiled. Other old soldiers in the crowd started to catch on, and a few of them told the people surrounding them.

"…point in the Kingdom." The Captain-of-the-Guard continued.

People started looking up as the word spread.

"…You are going to be…"

People started snickering as more and more of them caught on.

"…the new Sergeant-of-the-Tall-Tower!" The Captain-of-the-Guard said with great enthusiasm, making it sound very important. Kevin almost burst with pride right there in front of everybody, not really caring that he was not going to be the new Captain-of-the-Guard.

Everybody else almost burst out laughing right there behind Kevin. Except for the Captain-of-the-Guard, that is. He just frowned even more and to add emphasis to his frown he rolled his eyes too.

"Does that mean the Captain's not going to retire?" asked a confused voice.

"Nothing gets by you, does it?" answered a sarcastic voice.

The reason everybody wanted to laugh was Kevin's promotion meant Kevin would be unable to cause any more havoc in the village or anywhere else.

You see, the person selected to be the Sergeant-of-the-Tall-Tower, had to climb to the top of the Tall Tower. From there, it was his task to keep watch over the Kingdom, warn of an impending attack by an army or dangerous beast, and let the officers know if he saw any damsels in distress, odd or otherwise. I know that doesn't sound too bad, but the Tall Tower was so tall it took most people the better part of three hours to climb the narrow staircase to the lookout post. There is also the rule about the Sergeant-of-the-Tall-Tower having to stay at the top of the tower, because coming down from the tower would mean he had abandoned his post. The Sergeant-of-the-Tall-Tower abandoning his post would lead to thirty-seven slaps-in-the-face-with-a-wet-fish, and at least a week in the deepest cell in the dungeon. The very same cell used for those who dared to call King Archibald "Archie."

Mind you, it was still better than the previous punishment of fifteen, pokes-in-the-eye-with-a-sharp-stick. That punishment was stopped a long time ago, it was still an option if the person to be punished wanted, but as I mentioned earlier no one had gone for the poke-in-the-eye-with-a-sharp-stick option in a very long time. In fact, it had almost ceased to be an official punishment during the reign of King Archibald the XXIX (29), King Archibald's father.

Yes, I do realize that our King Archibald is the XXVIII (28), and normally would be Archibald the XXX (30), but for some strange reason the first King Archibald, Archibald the C (100), wanted to limit the number of Kings Archibald, so he decreed each subsequent King had to be one number lower than the previous one.

If the above still does not make sense after reading it a couple of times, do not worry, it is not that important. Kings being what they are, people with a lot of power, do not always have to make sense. A little bit like parents sometimes.

Anyway, Archibald the XXIX tried to stop the practice of poking-people-in-the-eye-with-a-sharp-stick because there were too many people wandering around with sore eyes and therefore could not do their work. Well, they could still work just not very well, so now it was a punishment that only the king could order. I do not advise you to try for yourself, as it is very painful.

It should be said here, the deepest dungeon was deeper than

the Tall Tower was tall. Therefore, abandoning the post at the top of the Tall Tower meant, at best, going up and down a lot of stairs, and having a sore face that smelled of wet fish.

Now you might be thinking the Sergeant-of-the-Tall-Tower could be relieved from time to time. The trouble was the Chancellor had made it abundantly clear there was only enough money for one Sergeant-of-the-Tall-Tower, add to that the fact there were very few, actually none, of the King's Guard who even for the briefest of moments thought about wanting to be a Sergeant-of-the-Tall-Tower.

You might also be wondering what had happened to the previous Sergeant-of-the-Tall-Tower. Nobody really knows, nor has anyone bothered to find out. The previous Sergeant-of-the-Tall-Tower had been locked up in the Tall Tower over thirty years before. After a few years, someone happened to look up and noticed that there was nobody keeping vigil over the Kingdom. That person thought about telling the proper authorities, but as he did not want to risk becoming the new Sergeant-of-the-Tall-Tower, he decided to leave well enough alone. When the proper authorities realized there was no longer a Sergeant-of-the-Tall-Tower in the Tall Tower, and there had not been anyone watching over the kingdom for some time, they decided not to say anything themselves, because they did not want to become the Sergeant-of-the-Tall-Tower, either.

While there was no Sergeant-of-the Tall-Tower, some crows moved into the top of the Tall Tower and seemed to be happy living up there, so no one felt like disturbing them. By the time Kevin came on the scene, almost everybody in the kingdom knew there was no longer a Sergeant-of-the-Tall-Tower in the Tall Tower but as no one wanted to replace the missing Sergeant-of-the-Tall-Tower, they all kept quiet. Someone had also started a rumor that if the crows were to leave the Tall Tower, terrible things would befall the Kingdom. Kevin did not know any of this. He was probably the only person in the kingdom who did not know any of this.

Kevin turned around, hoping to catch sight of his parents, to see if they had heard about his promotion. What he saw was a huge teary-eyed crowd. Kevin mistook their tears for tears of pride and joy. As you have probably gathered, Kevin was only half-right, they were very joyful, but the tears were due to them trying desperately not to laugh. Kevin's eyes began to brim with his own tears of pride, so he spun back around to face the Captain-of-the-Guard. Kevin spun so quickly that his already ill fitting helmet flew from his head. The Captain-of-the-Guard caught Kevin's helmet a fraction of a second before it hit him in the face. After Kevin had replaced his helmet, he looked up at the Tall Tower.

Kevin contemplated the tall tower for quite a while. At first he was excited to have such an important position in the king's guard but then he realized that it was a very, very, very tall tower and suddenly his insides felt very, very, very heavy. The thought of having to live at the top of the tall tower twenty four/seven was enough to make Kevin want to run, and run and run but the thought of the kingdom being deprived of a Sergeant-of-the-Tall-Tower, he decided, was even worse and he would just have to try and get used to being that far from the ground. Kevin was, if nothing else, very loyal to his country.

Once Kevin had decided that he would not run and hide from his new job he spent a little more time thinking along more practical lines.

"SIR! PERMISSION TO SPEAK, SIR." Kevin yelled. He had to yell, because by this time the crowd could not contain their laughter any longer. The laughter puzzled Kevin but as the Captain-of-the-Guard was either, still, or once again rolling his eyes and frowning, Kevin forgot about the laughter.

Kevin began wondering why it was the Captain-of-the-Guard liked rolling his eyes and frowning so much. Kevin then tried rolling his own eyes while frowning. It was too much for him and he lost his balance, causing him to fall onto a bunch of soldiers and villagers, well, he would have fallen on them if they had not suddenly parted and let him fall to the ground.

After getting back up and dusting himself off, Kevin saw the

Captain-of-the-Guard was trying, not very successfully, not to roll his eyes again but he was still frowning. The Captain-of-the-Guard inquired what it was Kevin had wanted to say before he had fallen over. Kevin asked, sensibly enough, if he were to be in the Tall Tower all day and night, how would he get food and water? The Captain-of-the-Guard thought for a moment, as he had not pondered this problem before.

The crowd fell silent.

"Well, er… um… I'll… have Grean-the-groper…"

"It's grocer, G.R.O.C.E.R., not groper. There is no P in grocer!" a voice yelled. It was Grean the groper… oops, I mean grocer.

One of the more comedic members of the crowd shouted, "Well you're not much of a grocer if you don't have any peas!" The rest of the crowd didn't think it very funny either so almost no one laughed, those that did tried to cover up their laughs by coughing, fooling no one.

"…arrange to have supplies brought up to you…" continued the Captain-of-the-Guard, frowning even more at the coughing.

Someone in the crowd started moaning. It was Grean-the-grocer's delivery boy.

"…once a week." The Captain-of-the-Guard continued, frowning and rolling his eyes, at Grean-the-grocer's delivery boy.

The moaning grew louder. The delivery boy was thinking about all the stairs that he would have to climb, carrying a very heavy basket of food and water every week.

When I say "delivery boy" I should probably add that Grean-the-grocer's delivery boy had started working at the grocery shop when Grean's grandfather first opened it, before Grean's father was born.

With that matter settled, Kevin bade his family farewell and momentarily wondered if his parents would miss having his help at the Big Bore Inn on his days off. Kevin need not have worried. In fact, Barry was thinking of the amount he would save in broken glasses, plates, spilled Brother Albert's Succulent Sustenance, etc. Barry even danced a little jig in celebration as Kevin ran off to collect his few belongings from the barracks.

KEVIN MEETS THE PRINCESS.

From a window in the dining room of his apartments, King Archibald watched the proceedings in the courtyard below with absolute disinterest; he had far more important matters on his mind. He turned to his wife, Queen Hortense.

Queen Hortense, sitting at the far end of the fifteen-foot long dining table, was enjoying her usual breakfast of scrambled eggs and toast with some bacon, sausage, fried potatoes, fried tomatoes, fried mushrooms and a small glass of fresh orange juice. She was, after all watching her weight.

King Archibald, all too familiar with his queen's excesses, watched as she shoveled yet another large spoonful of scrambled eggs into her mouth. Although quite hungry, King Archibald knew better than try taking a piece of toast from the stack next to the queen's elbow. The last time he had been tempted, Queen Hortense was enjoying a breakfast of pancakes and bacon, and eggs and so on. Naturally, the king had thought she would not miss one little pancake. He was wrong, very wrong. He was shocked at the speed his wife could move. Her spoon had smacked the back of his hand before he even touched the pile of pancakes!

For the billionth time King Archibald wondered, as he absent-mindedly rubbed the back of his hand, whatever happened to the beautiful, delicate girl he had fallen in love with so many years before. Then, for the billionth time, he remembered, she had run off with the stable boy, who, as it turned out, was really The Dastardly Pirate DeAmonté.

The Dastardly Pirate DeAmonté, after several years of marauding coastal kingdoms, decided to visit the landlocked King-

dom of Blognasee, where there were only rumors of his existence, for an extended vacation. As there were only rumors of his
existence, he felt quite safe that no one would recognize him or
even be thinking that he could be him. To ensure he would not
be recognized, he had disguised himself as a stable boy in King
Archibald's castle.

You might -as I did- wonder why a pirate, especially a prominent pitiless pirate, would want to work as a stable boy. I think he
just wanted to do something as different as possible from pirating, either that or he just loved being around horses, after all he
was born on a horse farm. As pirates do not have a lot of need for
horses while attacking other ships, he probably missed being
around horses.

One evening, The Dastardly Pirate DeAmonté was attending
the horse a certain beautiful, delicate girl had ridden to attend
a party at the castle. The party, thrown by King Archibald the
XXX (our King Archibald's grandfather), was to celebrate the
impending engagement of his grandson to a certain beautiful,
delicate girl. But, when she was helped down from her horse by
The Dastardly Pirate DeAmonté, and gazed into his eyes, she fell
instantly in love. Minutes later, they were riding off into the
sunset.

King Archibald snapped out of his reverie and realized he had
wandered closer to his queen and her breakfast.

"My darling petal…" King Archibald started just as Queen
Hortense spooned another generous helping of food into her
mouth.

"What?" She spluttered through a mouthful of food.

King Archibald wiped wet particles of scrambled egg, mixed
with bacon, tomato, and onions, from his face; he was surprised
by the onions, as he had not noticed them on the table before.

"We must decide what to do about our daughter. She is not
getting any younger, and nor are we and the people want…"

"Who gives a rat's doo-doo about what the people want?"
Queen Hortense did not like to be disturbed while eating.

"You're right as usual, beloved. I just want to see Maybel…"

"Who?"

"Our daughter, dear"

"Oh, her. What about her? FOOTMAN!"

A footman in a badly fitting uniform sauntered over from where he had been standing inattentively with two other footmen. As the footman wandered over to Queen Hortense, King Archibald could not help thinking to himself it would be really nice to have servants who knew how to act like real servants. Even nicer would be servants who knew how to act like real servants and fit into the uniforms they were given. He felt he must ask the Chancellor about that, sometime.

"You yelled?" said the footman in a very snooty manner.

"Bring me more food! I'm starving," ordered Queen Hortense.

"Starving the rest of the world," muttered the footman as he ambled out of the dining room to the kitchens.

King Archibald turned away from this pathetic picture and gazed out of the window just in time to watch Princess Maybel take her dog, Tiddles, for his walk.

King Archibald, sighed the sigh of a man who has almost given up. The sight of one's only offspring dragging the stuffed remains of a one-hundred-and-forty-three pound Rottweiler around the garden would make anyone sigh such a sigh.

When Maybel was told her faithful hound had died she cried for her beloved pet, as many people would. Unlike most people though, Maybel kept crying and moping around for a very long time. After six months of non-stop wailing and carrying on, it was decided Tiddles had made a miraculous recovery, insofar as Tiddles was not completely dead. Instead, it was determined that he was just… not quite as lively as before. Princess Maybel was, according to some of the servants, a few jewels shy of a tiara so she readily accepted that Tiddles was as happy as a lark being stiff as a board, and rolling around with his feet nailed to a lump of wood on little wooden wheels. That was five years ago. Tiddles was not wearing well, and had lost one of his hind legs and both ears.

"Stuffem & Goode", the local taxidermists, tried to replace

KEVIN MEETS THE PRINCESS. | 39

the hind leg with a sheep's but that too had fallen off. Princess Maybel still took Tiddles out for his daily walk and even threw sticks for him. The sticks were retrieved by one of the stable boys while another stable boy distracted Maybel.

King Archibald sighed again and turned from the window.

"My dear, we must find a suitable husband for our daughter." The King ignored the muffled giggling from the footmen.

"She can't marry just any old Prince. He must be brave, strong, handsome, intelligent, and above all…"

"Rich," added a footman.

"Like to eat green beans," added another.

The king, queen and other two footmen stared curiously at him, his face immediately, turned red with embarrassment.

"Like dead dogs," continued the first footman. At this, all three footmen burst into uncontrollable fits of giggling and collapsed to the floor.

"…PROVE himself worthy to become King of my people." finished the King glaring at the squirming pile of footmen.

"Well, if you hadn't had the last one thrown into the dungeon…" said Queen Hortense.

"He called me Archie," complained King Archibald.

"I call you Archie and you don't throw me into the dungeon."

The king stifled a small smile as he heard a footman giggle, "Like anybody could throw you an inch."

King Archibald resisted adding he would dearly love to have the footmen try throwing the queen into the dungeon. He was sure the act of throwing the queen into the dungeon would seriously hurt the footmen. Instead, King Archibald just said, as he always did when this came up,

"That's why, dear. I don't want just anyone calling me Archie."

This is of course what everyone called him. Not within earshot of the king mind you, and never to his face.

Queen Hortense fluttered her eyelashes coquettishly at the king. The queen's fluttering eyelashes reminded King Archibald of the crows living at the top of the Tall Tower. King Archibald shuddered; he did not like crows.

The real reason King Archibald did not like to be called Archie was the only other person to call him Archie was the beautiful delicate girl he had fallen in love with so many years before. That's right: the one who ran off with the stable boy who turned out to be The Dastardly Pirate DeAmonté on vacation.

King Archibald had tried a long time ago to let his queen know she should not call him Archie, but she had just laughed and playfully slapped him. The playful slap knocked him off the balcony they were standing on. During the six months in a body cast, which King Archibald had to endure as a result, he decided, when he recovered, he would give up trying to stop Queen Hortense from calling him Archie. He also decided that if anyone else called him Archie, the offender would be sent to the deepest dungeon forever.

The door to the dining room burst open and a tall thin man dressed in a beautifully tailored bright blue suit skidded into the room. King Archibald tried to ignore this commotion but, reluctantly, he turned to look at his Chancellor, Francis (Frank) Sterling.

The Chancellor's job is to take care of the finances of the kingdom. Frank, however, spent most of his time working on increasing his own financial well-being. He also loved bright colors and prided himself on always looking very dapper. He did not always get it right, most of the time his choice of color combinations was, at best, questionable and often downright wrong. Nevertheless, his clothes were always impeccably tailored.

King Archibald thought of telling Frank the bright blue suit, while impeccably tailored, really did not go well with his bright orange hair. He also contemplated telling the Chancellor nobody in the Kingdom, or elsewhere, thought the beehive hairdo was either fashionable or flattering to a tall thin person of any gender. Nevertheless, King Archibald, like almost everybody in the realm, preferred to minimize his dealings with the Chancellor whenever possible. That was until the Chancellor announced he had found the perfect suitor for Princess Maybel.

"Is he brave?" inquired the King.

"He's rich." Frank answered, rubbing his hands together.

"Is he handsome?" tried the King.

"He's very wealthy." replied Frank, licking his lips.

"Is he at least intelligent?"

"Did I mention that he has a lot of money?"

"Does he like dead dogs?" asked one of the footmen.

"Er… I don't recall asking," said the Chancellor.

King Archibald glared viciously at the footmen. The footmen did not see their king glare at them, as they were too busy giggling again.

King Archibald turned away from the Chancellor and looked out of the window.

"Make sure this prince of yours is properly received, and please find a new tailor for the footmen." He said dismissively.

Princess Maybel was returning from her walk with Tiddles just as Kevin was running to the Tall Tower. They met. That is to say, they bumped into each other. Kevin helped Princess Maybel to her feet as the stable boys righted Tiddles. Princess Maybel was not happy.

"You stupid little soldier! How dare you be running where I am walking? My Daddy will have you thrown into the dungeon and then he'll torture you until you're dead, then he'll kill you then, he'll… he'll… he'll…"

Kevin had fallen, fallen madly in love. She was the most beautiful girl he had ever seen. The less generous members of the king's household thought of Princess Maybel as rather homely, neither ugly nor stunningly beautiful, one might even have called her plain. She was also the first girl who had ever spoken more than two words to him.

Princess Maybel suddenly realized the soldier who had so rudely knocked her down was now rudely staring at her, and even more rudely, was drooling a little. The drooling reminded her of Tiddles when he was more lively. None of the princes her father tried to get her to marry had ever drooled at her. She stared at Kevin for a while and fell madly in love with him. He was after all almost handsome and he was the first person to, actually drool at her. It was a match made in heaven.

Back in the king's chambers the Chancellor was droning on and on about how hard it was to find a decent tailor for the servants with the budget he had been given, and how even the soldiers were starting to complain about the poor wages. King Archibald turned slowly away from the window, wondering what it was he had seen that disturbed him so. He muttered something about raising taxes then his head snapped back so fast his crown flew off his head. When the crown fell to the floor, little chips of gold paint flew off in several directions. Also, a couple of the jewels shattered, as though they were made of cheap glass. The Chancellor hurriedly cleaned up the mess and replaced the crown upon the king's head, hoping King Archibald had not noticed. The real crown (the one that had been made to replace the one stolen, allegedly stolen, by the dragon all those years before) had been sold to a passing merchant, who just happened to be selling a lot of bright blue cloth. The Chancellor need not have worried. The king had seen something far more disturbing to him. His darling daughter, his precious princess, was staring lovingly at some grotty little soldier who was drooling, a little, but drooling nonetheless. If there was one thing, besides people calling him Archie, King Archibald could not stand, it was common little people drooling in front of his dearest daughter.

Seconds after Kevin and Princess Maybel realized they had fallen helplessly in love with each other, Kevin was grabbed, by a pair of the bigger members of the King's Guard, and frog marched to the dungeons. The-Captain-of-the-guard had to take a leave of absence. His eyes had rolled so far back into his head, and his brow had creased so deeply upon hearing the news, that he could not get his eyes back again or even his brow straightened out.

PRINCE COLAH THE UNFORTUNATE.

On the other side of the mountain range, in the Kingdom of Keyannti, where King Reokha and his daughter, the beautiful Princess Lilien lived, a potentially very wealthy prince was trying to impress the king and princess.

The potentially very wealthy prince was Prince Colah the Unfortunate. Prince Colah the Unfortunate was so named... for many reasons but principally because he was not a handsome man; he resembled a very thin weasel, a tall, very un-furry weasel, with large ears and a few too many teeth. He also had a rather bad sense of smell (unlike most weasels) and insisted on wearing the cheapest and therefore most pungent, eau-de-cologne. Another reason he was known as Prince Colah the Unfortunate, was because his parents, shortly after he turned sixteen, made him leave their kingdom to find a bride. He was now twenty, and had been rejected by every prospective princess in the known world, some of them more than once.

The rejections came despite the fact Prince Colah had the potential to be very wealthy thanks to his father being very fortunate.

His father, King Fizzejinx, had made a large fortune by selling the formula for a special medicinal potion. The formula, as these things often happen, was "created" due to series of mishaps.

King Fizzejinx was an avid tinkerer of various things but he especially enjoyed mixing all sorts of peculiar powders. One day he was sorting through his growing collection of peculiar powders, when a small bird flew in through the open window. King

Fizzejinx put his cup of lemon sugar water (that was the popular beverage of those times) down on a shelf that was right below another shelf with a neatly arranged row of small glass vials on it. Each vial was filled with a brightly colored liquid. There were also a couple of packets of powder placed a little too close to the edge of the shelf.

As the good king tried gently to encourage the bird to fly back out of the window, he bumped the tray of freshly, and very finely ground spices a footman was bringing into the king's chamber. The tray flew into the air as did the powdered spices. A small cloud of fresh, finely ground spices formed and made its way into the generous nostrils of the footman. He, not surprisingly, sneezed, loudly. The loud sneeze shocked the king and scared the bird, who had just landed on the packets of powder precariously perched on the shelf. As the bird leapt from the shelf, and King Fizzejinx lunged at the bird, the packets of powder tumbled off the shelf and bounced off the rim of King Fizzejinx's cup below. The bird found the open window and flew away. When King Fizzejinx had lunged at the bird, he also bumped one of the vials of brightly colored liquid, which tipped over and bumped the one next to it and so on down the line. The small glass stopper popped out from one of the vials, spilling the bright green fluid inside, some of which dripped off the shelf and into King Fizzejinx's drink.

The footman's sneeze had not only scared the bird but also had created a bigger cloud of fresh, finely ground spices, causing both the footman and the king to begin, what sounded like, a sneezing competition. Due to the footman's exceptionally prominent facial feature, he was winning in both frequency and volume.

"Pinoch,.........try.........holding.........your.........hatchoofithzz.........nose." suggested the king.

Once the sneezing had subsided the king reached for his glass and took sip of his drink. Suddenly King Fizzejinx felt like being very generous and wanted to buy Pinoch the footman a ...a ...a? He equally suddenly could not remember what he wanted to buy the footman. King Fizzejinx took another sip of his drink and again felt like buying the footman a ...drink ...but not just any drink ...a drink just like... the one he was drinking!

King Fizzejinx became obsessed with discovering what had happened and exactly which potion had spilled into his lemon sugar-water, which of the finely ground spices and how much of each, had settled in his glass. He eventually managed to replicate the formula after a couple of years of experimenting.

There was a period where he had to endure some rather nasty tasting beverages and a few odd side effects. The third ear on his forehead, one of the oddest side effects, thankfully shriveled up and fell off after only a few weeks. The extra ear, along with some of the lesser side effects and the occasional strange tasting concoction, made it very difficult to find willing subjects to taste test the potions.

Once King Fizzejinx was able to reproduce the formula, sans side effects, he named the new potion after his son, Prince Andrew, who everyone called Prince 'Dew. It was Prince 'Dew's older brother Colah who first called Andrew, 'Dew, when they were a lot younger, Colah had been unable to say Andrew clearly at the time.

Shortly after the king was able to find a way of mass-producing 'Dew. Some very energetic people were visiting the kingdom, hoping to climb some of the local mountains. Incidentally King Fizzejinx's kingdom was called Sassparrill.

The energetic people were on a quest to find the perfect potion, a potion that would help them have the energy to climb mountains. When they tried, 'Dew, the energetic people immediately wanted to buy the formula for it. Prince 'Dew, being wise in the matters of business said they could only buy the right to make 'Dew and had to pay a small fee each time they sold a bottle of it.

Shortly after 'Dew was released to the public it became the only beverage anybody wanted to buy, either for themselves or for their friends. As a result, all of those small fees added up to a huge amount of money, so thanks to Prince 'Dew's cleverness, the Kingdom of Sassparrill rapidly became one of the richest in all of Paassda.

It was about that time that King Fizzejinx grew weary of his eldest son's choice of eau de cologne and apparent unwillingness to do anything. Prince Colah, unlike his younger brother Andrew, did not really contribute much to the running of the kingdom or anything. He was something of a "bump on a log."

King Fizzejinx decided Prince Colah should leave the kingdom of Sassparrill and broaden his horizons. If Prince Colah wanted to share the family fortune, all he had to do was to find a princess willing to marry him before he reached the age of twenty-four. Reluctantly Prince Colah agreed, he did admit to Prince Andrew that he was getting bored, he also thought that it would only take a couple of months.

Unfortunately, Prince Colah's quest was proving to be not as easy as he had hoped, which was not much of a surprise to those who knew him.

The kingdom of Keyannti was Prince Colah's fifteenth Kingdom. As his many attempts to woo the princesses had been failing so miserably, Prince Colah decided maybe he should try a different approach.

Prince Colah liked to read, mostly fairy tales and other fanciful stories. After many years and many stories, he realized the most successful princes had had to complete a dangerous task in order to gain the hand of the local princess.

A flash of inspiration came to him as he, along with his entourage were being escorted from the kingdom of Lyze. This was less than an hour after Princess Leila of Lyze had literally thrown Prince Colah out of her castle. Some of the Lyzean soldiers told Prince Colah there was rumored to be a dangerous beast roaming the countryside of Keyannti, terrorizing the people. They went on to add, King Reokha, the king of Keyannti, had decreed that whosoever rid his kingdom of the terrible beast would be awarded his daughter's hand in marriage. Prince Colah gathered all the information he needed to find and either capture or slay this marauding monster, and set off for the kingdom of Keyannti.

Unfortunately, for Prince Colah, the people of Lyze were living up to their name, and had not quite told Prince Colah the whole truth. They had succeeded in getting rid of Prince Colah though, much to the satisfaction of Princess Leila. Princess Leila however, did lose some sleep over the fact her people had lied to Prince Colah. It was very disappointing, as she had been trying so hard to end the association of the kingdom's name and the nasty habit of never telling the truth. On the other hand, she was so, so happy Prince Colah had finally left her realm.

So that is why Prince Colah was, confidently sitting astride his horse in the town square of Valpollychella, the main town in the kingdom of Keyannti. A large crowd of townspeople had gathered around an especially constructed platform upon which King Reokha and Princess Lilien, along with a few of the local dignitaries, were standing.

Prince Colah was looking very pleased with himself; he was thinking that it was a good sign that the people of Valpollychella had constructed a platform in the town center especially to receive him.

He did not realize the especially constructed platform was not for him, but had been built for the upcoming 600th anniversary of the kingdom of Keyannti. The especially constructed platform even had a huge banner, wrapped around the base of the platform, declaring the impending celebrations. Prince Colah was further encouraged when he noticed the logo for "'Dew" had been painted on the banner.

Of course, the logo was there not for Prince Colah's visit, but because the local "'Dew" factory was sponsoring the 600th anniversary celebrations.

The real reason King Reokha and all were gathered in the town square was because they were attending the dress rehearsal for the celebrations. It was by pure coincidence that Prince Colah and his entourage had arrived during a brief respite from the rehearsals.

Prince Colah's entourage consisted of about sixty-eight soldiers and servants. Most of the soldiers were on horseback too. The Prince motioned to one of his mounted soldiers to come forward as he addressed King Reokha.

"Sire, as you can see I have captured the terrible monster that was terrifying your good people, and as stated in the laws of your land, I claim the hand of the fair Princess Lilien as reward." declared Prince Colah with sincerity.

With that, the soldier, looking somewhat embarrassed, held up a rabbit. Not a big or even terribly mean looking rabbit, but a cute and cuddly white rabbit with a little pink nose and an even cuter, fluffy little bunny tail. The sort of rabbit, that would make almost any one squeal with delight. The rabbit began kicking furiously, trying to get away. Prince Colah screamed a little and tried to get his horse to back away from the rabbit.

"There. See? That is one ferocious rabbit look how it's trying to..."

"Prince ...um ...Prince, I..." began King Reokha.

Princess Lilien chose that moment to look up from examining her fingernails and let out an ear-piercing squeal of delight.

"Oh what a cute ickle, wickle, bunny-wunny!"

King Reokha turned and glared lovingly at his daughter, while everyone else slapped their hands over their ears trying to block out the squeal. All the local dogs started howling and barking. Even the rabbit seemed to be trying to cover its ears. Prince Colah became even more confused than usual and fell off his horse. His horse, quite used to this behavior, rolled her eyes. Prince Colah scrambled back up into his saddle only to realize he was sitting backwards. Prince Colah's entourage, quite used to this behavior, rolled their eyes.

Once Prince Colah was facing the right direction, King Reokha held up his hand for silence, since everyone on the platform and all of the townspeople were laughing so hard. Most of the Key-anntians could not remember a time when they had laughed as much as that day. When the laughter quieted down to a few uncontrollable giggles, King Reokha, barely containing his own mirth, resumed his reply to Prince Colah's demand for the princess' fair hand.

"Prince…? That is only a cute and cuddly rabbit, which I doubt could terrorize even the most sensitive of my subjects."

"Well it really put up a terrible fight." protested Prince Colah.

"Really?" asked the King.

"Yes. It took almost all of my men to capture it, and one of them sustained a nasty bite. So, when do Princess Lilien and I get married?" asked Prince Colah very sincerely.

"Never." answered the King just as sincerely.

"Wha… but I don't understand. I've just done you and your people a huge favor by capturing this dreadful monster, and you refuse to give me my just reward? This won't look good in the history books." tried Prince Colah.

"Listen very carefully …prince…?" Began King Reokha, "…for starters, I do not recall asking to be rid of a dreadful monster, as there has never been a report of any monsters, dreadful or otherwise, terrorizing my people. Then there is the minor detail you seemed to have missed, in the laws of this fair land. To be deemed worthy of my daughter's hand, and thereafter rule my people, you, single handedly, would have to have not only captured, but also slain any monster. Using your little rag-tag gang here, tends to violate that rule. So not only will I not let you marry my daughter but I am going to have you escorted from my kingdom, an experience I'm sure you are used to, and leave word that you are not to cross my borders ever again!" said the King, not hiding his disdain for this dolt of a prince.

"I'll let the rabbit go…" threatened Prince Colah.

"Please do. That way, it can chase you from my kingdom and save my soldiers the bother."

Prince Colah looked at the rabbit, looked back at the king, and then at the soldier holding the rabbit, then at the king, then the rabbit. He looked at Princess Lilien who chose that moment to squeal again.

"Oh Daddy, Daddy, Daddy, can I have the rabbit, can I, can I, please, Daddy, please Daddy?"

The look of total confusion on Prince Colah's face said it all.

Finally, the soldier holding the rabbit carefully put it down on the platform, and as soon as he let go of its ears, it hopped over to Princess Lilien who once again squealed with delight. The squeal was so intense that several nearby windows chose that moment to change into lots of small bits of glass and fall to the ground. Luckily, the townsfolk by this time had put their earplugs in, but the dogs still howled horribly. Prince Colah, surprisingly, did not fall off his horse this time.

The rabbit turned, smiled, and winked at Prince Colah with an evil glint in its eye. Of course Prince Colah was the only person to see this, as everyone else had turned away to head home. Prince Colah looked about him to see if anyone had seen the rabbit's smile, but all he saw was a troop of very competent looking soldiers surrounding his entourage. The soldiers then started mouthing something to Prince Colah, but for some strange reason the only thing he could hear was a strange ringing sound. The competent soldiers gave up trying to talk to the temporarily deafened prince. One of the soldiers grabbed Prince Colah's reins and escorted Prince Colah and all to the border. While on that journey, the soldiers of Keyannti kept making little jokes, about dangerous rabbits, how "brave" Prince Colah and his soldiers were and what a good rider Prince Colah was not.

King Reokha and the rest of his court left the specially constructed platform and climbed into their golden carriages to head back to his castle. King Reokha turned to the Princess Lilien and said.

"I wouldn't even wish that fool on poor King Archie and his daughter, what's her face?"

"Maybel. She might set her dog on him," replied Princess Lilien as she cuddled the cute white rabbit.

At that, they both laughed all the way back to the castle.

The rabbit twitched its little pink nose and settled into Princess Lillien's lap.

THE SCHOOL FOR WAYWARD PRINCES AND PRINCESSES.

About a year after Princess Maybel and Kevin had fallen help-lessly in love, only to be rudely and roughly separated, Prin-cess Maybel returned from the "School for Wayward Princes and Princesses."

Let me explain what the "School for Wayward Princes and Princesses" was and how it got started.

About two hundred years before our story starts, a half dozen or so very concerned kings and queens gathered together to dis-cuss a very troublesome problem. The very troublesome prob-lem was their princes and princesses were refusing to abide by tradition, and marry the prince or princess presented to them by their parents.

The kings and queens all felt it was more than reasonable for them to pick out the most suitable suitors for their sons or daughters, especially after they had spent many months, or in some cases many years, negotiating with the other set of par-ents as to how the two kingdoms would benefit from the glori-ous union of their kingdoms and offspring. Unfortunately, royal parental units did not take into account the feelings and wishes of the royal offspring, or even whether the princes or princesses concerned would like each other, which often they didn't, and therefore did not always live happily ever after.

The kings and queens chose to blame the popular media of those times, rather than accepting their children did not al-ways agree with them. The popular media of those times were the travelling storytellers, who roamed the land telling fanci-ful stories about princes and princesses making independent choices about who they should marry and so on. The stories often told of a prince or princess who had found true love by kissing a frog, falling asleep for a hundred years, putting the right sized shoe on a scullery maid, living with dwarves until the right prince came along, and so on. Most of the stories involved evil stepmothers or cruel kings and often there would be a wicked witch or wizard as well as some mythical beast, flying monkeys for example, thrown in for good measure.

A good witch, eccentric wizard, fairy godmother, cadre of compassionate dwarves or magical animals, usually helped the prince or princess in the stories. Even the woodland creatures lent a helping hand, or paw, beak, fluffy tail... some, mostly frogs, were transformed into the prince or princess of the main character's dreams, usually after being kissed.

At first the story tellers were welcomed into the castle or palace of the royal children, especially for birthday celebrations. As time passed however and the regal parents began paying attention to the stories, they decided to not hire any more storytellers. Instead they hired the local clowns who were far more likely to scare the kids. This lead to the royal rug rats realizing their parents did not always parent perfectly.

To make up for the loss of regal recompense the storytellers began entertaining the "ordinary" children with the same stories. This upset the kings and queens because the ordinary kids were trying on royal footwear at every opportunity. The storytellers were eventually banned from the castles and from telling certain stories in public, but small groups of princes and princesses would sneak off and go to a Tell-In.

At a Tell-In storytellers would gather the local kids, royal and ordinary, to tell them stories they were not allowed to tell. The Tell-Ins were often sponsored by the local fairy godmother or good witch, or the odd kindly dwarf (some of them were very odd). Most of the "common" grown-ups did not know about the Tell-Ins and those who did, did not think the stories were all that bad, after all "what harm can a little story do?" The nobility felt very differently but, typically, never bothered to explain the dangers, as they saw them, of a Tell-In to the common folk.

The majority of the Tell-Ins were, usually, held late at night in an old barn or storage building, sometimes they were held in a nearby wood or forest but never in the same place. For the most part only trusted people were invited to a Tell-In. Occasionally a guest had a hard time keeping the location secret. When the secret got out and the local king or queen became aware of a Tell-In happening in their neighborhood, they would dispatch their finest soldiers to raid the Tell-In. The soldiers' orders were to arrest the storytellers and any common folk, like scullery maids, stable boys, dwarves or frogs; and throw them into the nearest dungeon. As for any princes or princesses present, they were to be brought straight back to the castle and locked into a tower for a week.

The most successful raid netted two storytellers, a few scullery maids, half a dozen stable boys and about ninety-three frogs, but most of the other participants got away. As the scullery maids and the stable boys were all from the same castle and no one else wanted to do their jobs, they were allowed to go back to work. As punishment, they were made to pay for the privilege of working.

The storytellers were not so lucky, they were sent to the Island of Kiiddz, where the population was made up of very small people. The Kiiddeez, were rather peculiar, in that they had heard every story ever told so they only wanted to listen to their two favorite stories. Any storyteller, sent to the Island of Kiiddz, therefore had to tell the same two stories over and over and over, for the rest of their lives. Some storytellers had tried to escape by swimming back to the mainland but had not taken into account the giant mollusks and were never seen, or heard again.

Every now and then, the Tell-Ins would involve a spelldown between local witches. Often a good witch created a spell to hide the location of the Tell-In. When the local monarchy got wind of the Tell-In they would hire a local wicked witch to break the good witch's spell. The resulting fracas between the good and wicked witches was often spectacular, if not positively spellbinding. As I am sure you can imagine, in fact anything you can imagine happening, probably did happen. More often than not, it was the good witch who had to clean up, return the trees, woodland creatures and anything else back to their natural form. The busier good witches would send one of their trainees to clean up. These less experienced witches sometimes missed the odd transformation, like a prince that had been turned into a tree or a rock or frog even.

The hiring of wicked witches though, was always risky because sometimes they decided they had not been paid enough, especially if they were injured or had to use more potion than usual. If the local monarch failed to satisfy the demands of the wicked witch, they ran the risk of some very bad things happening to their kingdom and would then have to hire a good witch to dispel the evil enchantments. The situation could become extremely complicated and often led to the demise of the monarch. All of which made great fodder for the local storytellers.

The Tell-Ins began to die out soon after the invention of the printing press, which made it so much easier for the kids to get the stories. Ever since then, the rulers of the world have had an ever-growing and troubled relationship with the media.

Anyway, back to the "School for Wayward Princes and Princesses."

After a several years, and more princes and princess' making decisions of the heart by themselves, the kings and queens gathered together at a neutral location (which took several years to organize so none of them felt slighted) and founded the "School for Wayward Princes and Princesses." The location of the school, which was a closely guarded secret, also took several years to be decided.

A member of S.T.O.R.Y. (the Society for Tellers of Ripping Yarns) did manage to find the school but was caught before she could tell anyone the location. She was then forced to be the school's live in custodian to prevent her from revealing the school's location. As it was getting harder to make a living as a story teller she was quite happy. She was even happier to be able to surreptitiously tell stories to some of the students. She was eventually found out by the head of the school. The head of the school threatened to have the story telling custodian, escorted to the Island of Kiiddz. The custodian promised not to tell anyone anything about the whereabouts of the school or to ever tell another story to the students "Just don't send me to the Kiiddeez, please…" she had begged.

The school was staffed by the very strictest of traditionalists to teach the royal rug roamers about the realities of the privileged world the princes and princesses lived in, and what was expected of them by their doting parents.

In exchange for a life of being waited on hand and foot, not wanting for anything like food or clothing, fine or otherwise, the regal offspring were expected to perform some minor duties around their kingdoms. Duties like opening a new school, visiting people who were sick, sending the men of their realm off to fight battles, slay dreadful monsters, or rescue the odd damsel in distress here and there, and of course, marrying whomever their adoring parents picked out for them.

Usually the teachers were very successful, and the princes and princesses went home to marry the relevant prince or princess their parents had picked. Often, because the pair had already met and fallen in love at the school it was not a problem. All in all the school was a great success and almost every prince or princess had to spend at least a year there.

Until Princess Maybel that is. Despite their best efforts, the tutors had been unable to convince Maybel her love for Kevin was just a passing phase she would, and more importantly should, soon outgrow. Princess Maybel though, had been able to convince at least one instructor and three fellow students that true and instantaneous love could be found. The last time anyone heard from them, two of the students had run away to start a frog farm, and the other was learning how to clean floors with his true love. The instructor was seen galloping off into the sunset yelling something about finding the farm boy of her dreams.

The remaining teachers were successful in getting Princess Maybel to admit Tiddles had passed from the ranks of the living. They even had a little funeral service for him. Unfortunately, in the process, two more of the professors, who had been driven to distraction, had left the school muttering about finding the answer to life, the universe, and every little thing. The head teacher insisted, shortly thereafter, that Princess Maybel be returned to Blognasee, while there were still some teachers and students left.

When King Archibald heard the news of the educators' abject failure to dissuade Princess Maybel of her undying love for Kevin, and she was being "asked" to leave the school, he decided Kevin should be placed where Maybel would never see him again.

In the darkest cell in the deepest part of the dungeon, Kevin was chatting with his cellmate, a Prince Gaston, about the importance of not shortening somebody's name, especially a king's, when a pair of guards suddenly appeared and frog-marched Kevin out of the cell. Prince Gaston sighed heavily and once again asked the frogs in the next cell to keep the croaking down. His request, as usual, was ignored.

The guards hurriedly and very firmly marched Kevin straight up to the top of the Tall Tower and locked him in.

Now you might be wondering why King Archibald had Kevin sent to the Tall Tower. The king's reasoning was, he knew Princess Maybel had a very intense fear of heights, but not of deep dark dungeons. On the days when she was bored and all of her servants were, all of a sudden, very busy, she would go down to the dungeons and play with the prisoners. The prisoners at first protested, as they did not enjoy being dressed up in fancy dress and made to have little tea parties, especially as there was never any real tea or cakes. The mere thought of having a nice cup of tea and some warm, soft, moist cakes was torture enough, without having to pretend. Most of the prisoners, though, did not mind the dressing up, as it gave them a chance to wear clean clothes. The protests ended about a week after their usual meals of bread and water were replaced with meals of very thin air.

The day before Princess Maybel returned, the king issued a proclamation that no one in the kingdom was ever to mention Kevin within fifty miles of the princess. As most people had almost forgotten who Kevin was, this was not a difficult task.

That is, until the bell rang.

KEVIN'S NEW HOME.

The top of the Tall Tower had a room for the Sergeant-of-the-Tall-Tower. The room was roughly circular like the rest of the tower, and had a narrow balcony around it. The wall of the balcony was like the castle walls in that it also had crenellations. Inside the room were a chair, a table with only three and a half legs, a couple of thick books (they were being used as the top half of the fourth leg), and a wooden bed frame with the remains of a straw mattress. There was also a trapdoor in the floor, which was now locked from the other side, a door to the balcony, and two very grimy windows.

Above the Sergeant-of-the-Tall-Tower's room was the belfry (that's where bells are kept, especially large ones). The bell had been placed in the belfry for the Sergeant-of-the-Tall-Tower to ring in case of invasion or other such emergency. Attached to the bell was a length of rope for the Sergeant-of-the-Tall-Tower to pull in order to ring the bell.

The new Sergeant-of-the-Tall-Tower, Kevin, at first had to share his new quarters with about thirty-eight crows who were none too pleased to be suddenly sharing their limited space. The crows that were most upset occupied the remains of the straw mattress where they had made some very comfortable nests. Kevin was none too pleased at being shoved unceremoniously through the trapdoor into a crowd of cantankerous crows and a flurry of feathers.

The crows, after giving Kevin a few parting pecks, flew off in a furious flock, cawing their sentiments very loudly. The loud cawing drew the attention of those few Blognassians who believed in the stories of evil befalling the kingdom if the crows ever left the Tall Tower.

When they saw the crows leaving, they began to speculate on what would happen. After a day or two and no major catastrophes had befallen the realm, most of the villagers forgot about the legend. Some did not. They were the ones who blamed any minor mishap, like losing one of their socks in the wash or a tooth falling out, on the departure of the crows. They were also the people who believed in all the stuff about not-so-evil-wicked-witches and magical roses.

A few of the more determined believers stayed hidden in their cellars for at least another few days or until their supply of rose wine or beer ran out, in most cases though, that happened within a few hours of them going into the cellar. The fact they had run out of rose wine or beer, to them, was disastrous enough and was blamed on the crows leaving, which in a way was true.

Once Kevin had brushed the dust and stuff from his clothes, he looked around his new quarters, which took all of five seconds, and thought it could do with a little cleaning. Crows, it seems, do not have very good housekeeping habits.

Kevin, after discovering he was locked into the room at the top of the Tall Tower and the last of the crows had left, decided to make the best of a bad situation and clean up the mess.

The first thing Kevin tried to do was to get rid of the nasty dangly thing in the middle of the room. Kevin did not know about the very large and very heavy bell over his head as no one had told him about it. There used to be a sign attached to the bell-rope that read, "Do Not Ring Unless There Is An Emergency." However, the sign was no longer attached to the rope; it was buried beneath at least three inches of dust, discarded feathers, and crow poop.

The reason no one had told Kevin about the bell was only a few of the very old soldiers could remember there was one. It had not occurred to anyone to ask the old soldiers, nor did it occur to the old soldiers to tell anyone about the bell.

Kevin tugged at the rope gently; it did not budge. He tugged again, a little harder. Nothing happened. Kevin tugged even harder. Nothing. Kevin jumped and held onto the rope, and for a few seconds swung gently back and forth. There was a creaking from above and suddenly a lump of rotting rope fell on top of Kevin, Kevin fell to the floor. A very large very heavy bell and some bits of wood soon followed the rope.

As the floor of the Sergeant-of-the-Tall-Tower's room had been exposed to the caustic effects of crow poop and the elements for a very long time, it decided, a split second after Kevin landed on it, to move away in a distinctly downward direction. Kevin followed the floor, as did everything else. Kevin, as he fell down the seemingly empty center of the Tall Tower, looked up at the silhouette of the bell following him and wondered what was going to happen next.

The ceiling of King Archibald's bathroom just happened to be the next thing below the floor of the Sergeant-of-the-Tall-Tower's room. While Kevin was cleaning his new accommodations, King Archibald was enjoying a nice hot bath. King Archibald had just stepped out of his nice hot bath so he could yell at someone about the awful clanging sound that seemed to be getting louder, when Kevin landed in the king's nice hot bath. Kevin had dropped through a brand new hole in the, luckily for Kevin, poorly constructed ceiling. Before the king could think of what to yell at Kevin, Kevin and the king's bath, now only half-full of dirty soapy water, exited the king's bathroom. They did not exit through the door but through a bath shaped hole that appeared a microsecond later and just before a large clanging thing entered the bathroom, and promptly left again through a bell shaped hole. The king gingerly inched toward the new, large bell shaped hole in his bathroom floor. He looked down into the hole and watched as his bath, closely followed by Kevin and the bell, crashed their way down, all the while gathering more bits of floor and furnishings, to the dungeons. Then the king looked up at his new bell shaped skylight. King Archibald liked the new skylight, but was not happy about the new bell shaped hole in the floor of his bathroom. He was also upset about losing his bath.

Prince Gaston on the other hand, was quite pleased to see Kevin again and thanked him for the new, if somewhat damaged furniture and the fresh supply of firewood. He was not sure how he was going to get the guards to agree to allow a plumber to set up the new, if somewhat dented, bath. A very damp and dirty Kevin had just leapt out of the bath, still clutching the length of rope, when a second or two later a large bell enshrouded the bath.

Prince Gaston was not happy that his cell had grown considerably smaller due to all the new furnishings and there was now a large cast-iron bell shaped object covering the bath. Before Kevin had refurnished the cell, Prince Gaston could do a few exercises like push-ups and jumping jacks and so on, but now he would have to think up some new calisthenics he could perform in a much smaller space. The frogs just croaked even louder, much to the annoyance of Kevin and Prince Gaston.

The timing of this incident was unfortunate for the Captain-of-the-Guard. He had, only a week before, returned to duty, and had thought he had broken his habit of rolling his eyes and frowning. The doctors decided he should retire and employ a "seeing eye" dog, as his eyes had rolled so far back into his head they got lost.

After an extensive search of about four minutes, a new Captain-of-the-Guard was appointed. This upset the young Lieutenant, as he was passed over for a second cousin of King Archibald's. The second cousin's mother had been nagging the king for a long time about giving her son a better job. The nagging had not stopped, even after the king had his aunt thrown into the dungeon for six months. The six months in the dungeon had just given her more time to think of more ways to nag the king.

The new Captain-of-the-Guard was congratulated, very briefly, by the king and told to make sure, after the repairs to the tower had been completed, that Kevin would be once again confined to his new post.

A few weeks later, Kevin was once again dragged from the relative comfort of his cell up the new stairs of the Tall Tower and shoved, very unceremoniously, through the new trapdoor at the top of the tall tower. The first thing Kevin noticed about his refurbished room was someone had repaired the floor, rebuilt the belfry, and replaced the bell with a smaller lighter bell.

Rusty-the-blacksmith was very proud of the bell; he had spent a lot of time trying to come up with a new lighter metal than the cast iron of the previous bell. Rusty-the-blacksmith named the new metal after his newborn son Alan and the fact that its weight was so negligible. The new alloy was therefore called Alanminimum. The rope was new too.

A few floors below, the King was enjoying his nice new bathroom. The nice new bathroom was one of the two reasons the King had not had Kevin thrown into the deepest dungeon forever. The other reason was King Archibald was having a hard time keeping Maybel from rushing down to the dungeons to be with her true love.

Kevin settled into his new quarters fairly quickly, and was glad the people who had fixed the floor had also put in a pulley system. Now, every Monday morning, he could haul up his food and water for the week. Grean-the-grocer was even more pleased, and his delivery boy (the one who had done all the moaning earlier) was ecstatic, as he no longer had to climb all those stairs carrying a heavy basket of food and water to the top of the Tall Tower. Not that he ever had had to do so, as Kevin had not managed to spend more than a couple of hours at the top of the Tall Tower.

For the first six weeks of his stay in the tower, Kevin was excited at the prospect of being the first person to warn of an attack by anybody or anything. He was also glad of the fresh air after being in a stuffy dungeon. He did miss Prince Gaston's company. More so, he missed the nights when Princess Maybel was able to sneak down into the dungeons so they could discuss their plans for the future. At each visit, it became even more obvious their love for each other was no mere passing fantasy but the stuff of legend, and no matter what, they would be together.

That knowledge helped Kevin through some of the very lonely times at the top of the Tall Tower.

Kevin did not miss the croaking frogs and as the crows had all gone he did not have to listen to their constant cawing or put up with the persistent pecking.

Kevin diligently kept watch over the Kingdom, making sure to look out from every possible angle as often as possible. At first, he would do this on the run, running around and around the round balcony. The only trouble with running around a round balcony is after a while one will become quite dizzy. Kevin started to walk around the round balcony instead but he found he became just as dizzy, only it took longer.

Life in the village stayed pretty much the same. The merchants came and sold their wares in the market. The villagers came and purchased their provisions from the merchants. The horses and other large animals did what they had to do. The roses kept growing and as the invention of the internal combustion engine was still a long way off, the air stayed nice and fresh.

Every other day the soldiers would gallop out of the castle and practice their fighting and so on. As Kevin watched from the tower, it started to dawn on him that maybe the soldiers, who had told all those stories of daring do in his father's inn, had not been totally truthful. He could clearly see they never actually fought off any attacking armies or slew any dreadful monsters, let alone rescued any damsels in distress, odd or otherwise.

After a few months of nothing happening, Kevin started to grow bored, so he opened up one of the books that were still being used to prop up the little table in his quarters. Interestingly, it was a copy of Hyacinth McThornbush's "The Magical Properties of Roses." Kevin became engrossed in the book and once he finished "The Magical Properties of Roses.", he read the other book, a fanciful tome about dragons, supposedly written by a legendary dragon hunter whom Kevin had never heard of. When Kevin had read both books a couple of times he began asking for other books to be sent up with his food. It soon became common for the villagers to look up and instead of seeing

Kevin dizzily walking around the top of the Tall Tower; they would see him sitting on the parapet reading a book. Occasionally he would look up and make sure everything was all right in the Kingdom. The books also helped Kevin to feel no matter what, he and Maybel were destined to and would be, together. He also learned to conquer some of his fears, especially his fear of heights.

At this point, you might be wondering what had happened to Princess Maybel. King Archibald had tried insisting the "School for Wayward Princes and Princesses" take her back, but the school made it very clear to King Archibald that the school would rather close than allow Princess Maybel within a mile of the school grounds, as there were very few teachers or students left. Therefore, King Archibald sent Princess Maybel off to a finishing school instead, hoping that while there she would forget about Kevin.

A "Finishing School" is a school where young ladies from well to do families, are sent to learn the finer points of living a life of luxury. This means they learn how to make sure their servants know how to lay the table properly, mix drinks correctly, and carry the shopping, after a hard day at the market place. There were other lessons in essential skills for high-society ladies, like being able to walk while carrying books on their heads, dancing, how best to snub a rival or even how to discourage common folk from approaching them. Princess Maybel learned all of this and a lot more.

When Frank Sterling, the Chancellor, very excitedly, informed King Archibald that the prince he had spoken of a couple of years earlier, was now heading towards the Kingdom of Blognasee, King Archibald had Princess Maybel brought home. He forgot to tell anyone, especially Princess Maybel, there was a potential suitor coming. This lapse in memory led to a very embarrassing situation for the whole kingdom, which could have been a lot worse.

WEDDING PLANS ARE MADE.

One sunny day, about a week after Princess Maybel returned from the finishing school, Kevin looked up and saw something he had never seen before, a big cloud of dust on the horizon. Kevin watched the cloud get closer and soon saw what appeared to be large cloud of dust riding on several horses. Sensibly enough, Kevin thought it was an attacking army or possibly a monster; it definitely was not an odd damsel in distress. It would have to be a very odd damsel in distress. Of course, Kevin had never seen an attacking army before and the absolute lack of training he had received on how to recognize an attacking army did not help. What did help was the book on monsters he had read, which listed most of the known monsters, mythical or otherwise. Horse riding dust clouds were not on that list.

After watching the horse riding dust cloud for a while he concluded it must be an attacking army. Kevin fell off the wall in a state of semi-panic. Luckily, he fell onto the balcony and not down to the ground, which would have really hurt. He ran to the rope and began frantically ringing the bell.

At first, there was no reaction from below. It had been so long since anyone had heard the bell being rung, they had forgotten what it was for. Then suddenly the new Captain-of-the-Guard was yelling up at Kevin from a crowded courtyard. Kevin did not hear the Captain though, because he was ringing the bell.

Kevin was surprised to see the trap door flung open and a breathless soldier crawl up the last few steps into the room. Kevin stared at the panting heap of loose clothing and slowly realized it was pointing to the wall. Kevin stopped ringing the bell, went to the wall, and looked down. When the Captain-of-the-Guard saw Kevin, peering over the parapet, he whispered something to Kevin. The Captain-of-the-Guard was not whispering intentionally. He had been shouting so hard he had lost his voice. It did not help that, because of the bell being so loud, all Kevin could hear was a dull ringing sound.

The soldier who had been panting on the floor got up.

"Why ...did ...you ...ring ...the ...bell?" he panted.

Kevin stared blankly for a second, wondering why the Captain's lips were not moving and yet he could almost hear him speak. Kevin just about jumped over the wall when the panting soldier tapped him on the shoulder.

"Why did you... ring the bell?" he gasped again.

Kevin stared at the soldier with a very puzzled expression. Luckily, the soldier was fairly bright and realized that Kevin could not understand because of the bell, so he mouthed the words in an exaggerated fashion. A look of clarity crossed Kevin's face. Kevin pointed in the direction of the dust cloud.

The dust cloud was, by now, less than three miles from Lassaggnee. The soldier shouted to the Captain-of-the-Guard and he in turn yelled, or rather tried to, at his Lieutenant. The Lieutenant finally understood the message after the Captain-of-the-Guard scratched it in the dust of the courtyard. The Lieutenant then yelled the instructions to the Sergeant-at-Arms, who yelled instructions to the soldiers to get ready to defend the castle.

As they had done so much practicing, every soldier knew exactly what to do and did it. Soon the walls were lined with heavily armed soldiers ready to fend off the attacking army. The gates were slammed shut and, after much grunting and groaning, the portcullis was dropped. After even more grunting and groaning, the drawbridge was raised, much to the surprise of the young couple sitting on the side of the drawbridge, who fell into the foot or so of murky water and rubbish at the bottom of the moat.

Each of the narrow windows in the towers had an arrow poking out in the general direction of the marauding army. Unfortunately, the pretty lace curtains the ladies of the castle had put over the narrow windows became entangled with many of the arrows, frustrating the archers.

The attacking army was a little surprised to have the drawbridge raised just as they reached it, but they were even more surprised to be greeted by a shower of lace-adorned arrows. The attacking army was pleasantly surprised the lace-adorned arrows just bounced off them. Because the attacking army was busy being relieved about the lace adorned arrows bouncing off them, they ignored the damp young couple, both of whom were trying to free themselves from the gooey mud and rubbish at the bottom of the moat.

The lace-adorned arrows bouncing off the attacking army was, as it turned out, very fortunate. Not for the Sergeant-at-Arms, whose duties included making sure the soldiers had the correct weapons for any given situation. Soon after the incident, he spent a long time in the dungeons, chatting with Prince Gaston and the frogs, about the merits of having two sets of arrows, a blunt set for practice and a sharp one for actual fighting. Moreover, an essential part of the training should include instructing the soldiers which set of arrows they should use for each scenario.

As it turns out, Kevin and his total lack of skill with any weapon had prompted the procurement of the blunt arrows.

Prince Gaston, while grateful for the company, did keep trying to get the Sergeant-at-Arms to use the bath, as he smelled rather badly of fish. The Sergeant-at-Arms had, had to suffer a slap-in-the-face-with-a-wet-fish for each arrow, luckily for him the supply of wet fish ran out after the first forty-six slaps.

The incident with the blunt arrows was, however, fortunate for almost everyone else because the attacking army turned out to be Prince Colah the Unfortunate and his entourage.

Having failed so miserably in the Kingdom of Keyannti and a few other kingdoms since, mostly due to the rapid re-telling of a story concerning a certain "monstrous" rabbit, Prince Colah was forced to try the Kingdom of Blognasee. Prince Colah knew

King Archibald had a reputation for being a tyrant and the kingdom of Blognasee was by far the least wealthy kingdom in the whole of Paassda.

Prince Colah was also getting homesick and running very short of cash. It costs a lot of money to travel with such a large entourage. There is all the food that has to be bought, and veterinary fees, not to mention the hotels and wear-and-tear on clothing. He was also very close to his twenty-fourth birthday and therefore running out of time. In other words, King Archibald's kingdom and Princess Maybel were Prince Colah the Unfortunate's last hope.

Prince Colah the Unfortunate was King Archibald's last hope, as he had all but given up on finding a prince that he felt was worthy of his daughter's hand, or one that was even interested in her. More importantly, he wanted a prince he could control, as he did not want to give up the reins of his realm and as the Chancellor kept mentioning the "potentially very wealthy" part of Prince Colah's description, King Archibald's potential objections melted away.

The marriage was arranged with amazing speed, thanks in part to the negotiating skills of Frank Sterling, the Chancellor. After the deal was settled Frank spent most of his time wandering around with a greedily gleeful expression on his face and kept rubbing his hands together as though caressing a pile of gold coins. He was also frequently heard muttering to himself about how he was going to spend all the money that without doubt, would pour into the kingdom after the wedding.

Princess Maybel had tried to protest to her father that her husband-to-be was not quite, what she expected, anyway she was in love with Kevin.

Her father reminded Princess Maybel he was her father and knew what was best for her.

Princess Maybel tried to remind her father she was now eighteen and could make her own decisions, and Kevin was the true love of her life.

King Archibald went on to explain, as Princess Maybel was

still living in his castle she should do as she was told, including not fall in love with every little soldier that drooled at her.

Princess Maybel tried to explain it had been only one little soldier who had drooled at her, and anyway none of the princes he had tried to get her to marry had ever drooled at her and that Kevin was going to be her husband.

The king then explained to his daughter, she would be much wiser to return to her room, forget about "that pipsqueak of a drooling soldier" and prepare herself for her marriage to Prince Colah, "Who is a *real* prince!" or else he would get very angry indeed and just might take his anger out on "that pathetic little drip of a …a …a …whatever, just go to your room!".

Maybel went to her room and sulked.

The wedding plans went ahead.

Princess Maybel's wedding dress was a huge white gown made of the best silks Frank Sterling could find. The dressmaker, Sue Inng, knew it was not really made of silk. Only after the Chancellor had given Sue half of the money he had saved by buying fake silk, did she stop making little threats about life in the dungeon, without the possibility of fresh clothes, along with daily slaps-in-the-face-with-a-wet-fish, for stealing from the king.

The best orchestra to be had, for very little money, (another money saving ploy by the Chancellor, after all he had to pay for his new outfit somehow) was hired and given copies of the Blognasee national anthem, so they could practice.

A huge tent was erected in a field just outside the castle walls and adorned with thousands of roses. The castle was scrubbed clean and repainted. The footmen, soldiers, and even the stable boys were given new uniforms. The uniforms did not fit very well still, but at least they were new.

The village population doubled, then tripled and almost quadrupled as more and more people came to see the wedding. There were a lot of representatives from other kingdoms who had been sent by their respective royals to make sure, first that there was a wedding and second that it was actually Prince Colah the Unfortunate marrying Princess Maybel. There were so many fanciful stories floating around Paassda, about Prince Colah the Unfortunate, the task of verifying them was now a full time job for many people.

The swelling of the population of Lassaggnee, made Barry very happy, the rest of the villagers did not protest too much either, as now every spare room and even a few broom closets were being rented for five times the normal rate. Rusty-the-blacksmith was happy too, as there were lots of horseshoes that needed to be replaced after all those long journeys. The horses were happy because they got nice new lightweight horseshoes, as Rusty-the-blacksmith was using Alanminimum.

So everyone was very happy.

Well, almost everyone.

At least, two people were very unhappy.

Until the appearance of Millicent, that is.

MILLICENT.

Millicent was a rather large, iridescent green dragon with orange spots on her wings. Her tail was rather unique because the end was shaped something like a flat arrowhead with sharp spikes around the edges. Millicent had been dormant for eighty-four years, which coincidentally was when the last person to enter the part of the mountain range, where the dragons were rumored to live, entered but did not return.

Dragons are normally only dormant for seventy-seven years, but Millicent was a particularly lazy dragon. Nevertheless, even lazy dragons have to eat, and Millicent decided it was time to find something to satisfy her growing hunger. She was also feeling bored with her usual diet and a little lonely. It was purely by accident that she chose the day before the big wedding to leave her cave to seek out some company and suitable sustenance.

Kevin was watching the preparations for the wedding when something caught his eye. He looked up just as a huge ball of fire curled up into the clear blue sky above the Dark and Scary Forest. It was then he saw Millicent flying over the old village very near the place where the dragons were rumored to live.

Millicent was getting tired, very disappointed, and more than a little angry. Normally when dragons fly over a village, the inhabitants run in every direction and are pretty easy to catch. The people in this village, however, just stayed in their homes, even when she started to burn the houses.

It slowly began to dawn on her -lazy dragons, like lazy people, tend not to be too bright– maybe the village was no longer inhabited. Then she remembered this particular village was the one she came to the last time she had gone hunting for food, some eighty-four years ago. Exhausted and now even hungrier, after expending all her energy, a very disgruntled Millicent flew back to her cave to rest. Millicent did grab a snack on her way back to her cave, but even though the forest had plenty for her to eat, she really felt like eating something different.

Kevin, never having seen a dragon before except in pictures, stared in amazement. As he watched the huge creature fly away towards the mountain range, it struck him he should probably tell somebody.

He dropped the huge book he was reading and fumbled for the bell rope, trying not to take his eyes off the creature. Eventually he had to turn around to find the rope so he could ring the bell.

The Captain-of-the-Guard used the new communication tube that ran up the side of the Tall Tower to find out what was wrong. Kevin told him about the dragon. The Captain-of-the-Guard called to the other lookouts in the other towers and asked if they had seen the dragon. Three of the towers had an obstructed view of the area, so the guards on those towers reported they had not seen any dragons. The fourth guard did have a good view of the area but had been asleep and only woke up after hearing the commotion below. He peered into the distance but saw nothing, which is what he told the Captain. Kevin was told to stop daydreaming and disturbing everyone.

Kevin sulked.

When Princess Maybel heard some of the footmen laughing about the "...phantom dragon Kevin had dreamed up..." she asked the king if the wedding would be cancelled. She was told, very clearly, the wedding plans would not be slowed down one millisecond, particularly for some non-existent dragon.

Princess Maybel sulked.

The footmen were each given fifteen slaps-in-the-face-with-a-wet-fish, for mentioning Kevin's name near the princess.

The footmen sulked.

When it was pointed out they would receive another round of slaps-in-the-face-with-a-wet-fish, they stopped sulking and went back to work.

That night Millicent was awakened by her copious stomach gurgling loudly. Feeling even hungrier than before, she decided to try to find a midnight snack.

The next morning, the day of the wedding, Kevin saw smoke rising from a farm only a couple of miles from the castle. Kevin reported to the guard who had been assigned to wait by the communication tube in case there was anything to report. Kevin had been told to only ring the bell if the castle was in imminent danger.

The guard reported to the Sergeant-at-Arms, who had been released from the dungeon that very morning. The Sergeant-at-Arms reported to the Lieutenant, who reported to the Captain-of-the-guard. The Captain-of-the-Guard told the Lieutenant to tell the Sergeant-at-Arms to tell the guard to tell Kevin, to only tell the guard to tell the Sergeant-at-Arms to tell the Lieutenant to tell the Captain-of-the-Guard when Kevin had something important to tell the guard to tell the Sergeant-at-Arms to tell the Lieutenant to tell the Captain-of-the-Guard, as he (the Captain-of-the-Guard) was not interested in careless farmers burning down their own farmhouses.

Kevin sulked.

The farmer, luckily for him, having been woken up by a series of tremendous popping sounds, rushed out of his farmhouse in time to see Millicent swooping down on his farm. The farmer grabbed his family and bundled them down into the cellar. The next morning he went to inspect the damage and found that his corn crop was destroyed, all that was left were a few puffy white things scattered across the charred field.

The farmer sulked.

Millicent, however, had still not satisfied her hunger and decided to fly over the big village with the castle near it, especially as it seemed to have a lot of people milling about in the big field behind the castle. Luckily for Kevin and Princess Maybel, Millicent did her first fly-by, a couple of hours before the wedding ceremony was due to start.

Kevin was still sulking and so was not doing his job. He was sitting on the floor in his room at the top of the Tall Tower, reading yet another book and refusing to look out over the Kingdom. He had a vague impression of something very big and very scaly flying past his tower. When he heard the screams from below, he dropped the book, ran out of his room and looked out over the parapet. At first, he saw nothing but he did hear a huffing and flapping sound.

Kevin turned just in time to see Millicent flying straight at his tower. Kevin dove for cover as Millicent's huge tail crashed into the roof of the tower, which along with the bell, and his ever-growing collection of books, crashed down on top of Kevin. Millicent howled in pain.

The people on the ground screamed even louder, as they thought the huge beast was roaring just before attacking them. They all ran in different directions, but most of them ran into the castle, slamming and locking all the doors shut.

On the bandstand outside the big tent, King Archibald had been trying to get the orchestra, the Chancellor hired, to play the Blognasee national anthem. The King was beginning to think each member of the orchestra was either totally tone-deaf or had absolutely no musical ability whatsoever. He had just managed to get them to play the first few notes of the anthem, which King Archibald had written, at the same time and almost in the same key, when they all, inexplicably and very suddenly, ran off.

The King hung his head in frustration and failed to notice everybody else had suddenly, and equally inexplicably, disappeared. Then the King saw the dragon's shadow as she flew overhead. Within a split second, the King was trying to gain entry into his castle. This was not an easy task, as the people who had already escaped to the sanctuary of the castle had locked all the doors. The three footmen were on the other side of the door the King was trying to enter.

"Open the door!" yelled King Archibald.

"No!" yelled the first footman.

"You didn't say the magic word," trilled the second footman

"What?" demanded King Archibald, not believing his ears.

"Didn't your mother teach you to say please?" asked the third footman in a really snooty voice.

"Open the door and let me in. Now!" King Archibald was getting extremely angry.

"Not unless you say please," said the second footman.

"Please open the door?" King Archibald asked as nicely as he could. He was trying to calm himself by imagining what he was going to do with the three footmen when he got back into his castle.

"Are you still there?" the first footman asked, sounding surprised.

"Yes. Now for the last time…" started King Archibald

"Go away; we're not letting anyone in. King Archie's orders," interrupted the third footman.

This was true. The king, or at least one of the previous Kings Archibald, had ordered, in the case of an emergency such as a large hungry dragon flying about, no one was allowed to enter the castle once the doors were closed.

"Let me in!" yelled King Archibald again.

"You can yell all you want, we're not letting you in," said the third footman in an even more snooty voice than before.

"For the last time LET ME IN!" King Archibald was beyond ordinary anger now.

"No." the footman said firmly.

"If you don't let me in, I'll have you thrown in the dungeon," King Archibald threatened.

"No," came, the stubborn reply.

"Just be good little dragon fodder and go away," said the snooty footman.

"Last chance before I bring back poking-in-the-eye-with-a-sharp-stick, to go along with the three hundred slaps-in-the-face-with-a-wet-fish you're each going to get." King Archibald had managed to calm himself somewhat by imagining the footmen being poked-in-the-eye-with-sharp-sticks and then slapped-in-the-face-with-wet-fish, or even both at the same time. A truly cruel and unusual punishment.

"Oh right, like you're King Archie," said the first footman.

"Only King Archie can reinstate pokes-in-the-eye-with-a-sharp-stick, not some sniveling little..." began the second footman.

"Look through the peephole," interrupted King Archibald quietly.

There was a long silence.

The cover of the peephole slid to one side.

A green eye appeared.

King Archibald glared at it.

The green eye blinked, twice and disappeared.

A blue eye appeared and blinked.

King Archibald glared at that eye, too.

The blue eye disappeared.

The cover of the peephole slid back into place.

There was some more silence.

There was the sound of a scuffle.

The cover of the peephole slid open and a small grey eye appeared.

King Archibald glared again.

The small grey eye seemed to grow as it recognized King Archie.

Once again, the peephole was closed.

Once again, silence.

Once again sounds of a scuffle on the other side of the door.

Then there was the sound of rusty bolts being drawn back.

There was the sound of many locks being unlocked.

More silence.

King Archibald gently pushed the door open and stepped into an empty hallway, a very long empty hallway, with one door at the far end. He walked along the empty hallway. When King Archibald came to the door at the end of the hallway, he opened it. On the other side of the door were a sparsely furnished room and another door. King Archibald walked through the room, opened the door, and walked into another sparsely furnished room with yet another door on the other side. King Archibald walked through this room and through a good many more rooms. All the rooms were very similar in that each was sparsely furnished and totally void of people. Eventually King Archibald reached the main staircase and climbed up the stairs to yet another long hallway with a door at the far end. King Archibald walked toward the door at the far end, but stopped before he reached it. He turned, looked behind him, and then looked at the door he was standing in front of and opened it. The door he was standing in front of led into the throne room. The throne room was not empty. The throne room was full of people trying to act as though they had always been part of the royal scene.

The three footmen came running over to King Archibald.

"Your highness, you're safe. Thank G…"

"Guards, throw these fools into the dungeon and get some fish and sticks."

As the guards carried the protesting footmen out, the King walked slowly through the crowded room. Everybody avoided his glare. Even the Queen, but she was busy stuffing her face full of some fish and chips that a guard had just brought. King Archibald too focused on something else, failed to notice that the guard had not brought the fish and sticks that he had ordered.

King Archibald looked around and saw Prince Colah's feet poking out from underneath one of the tapestries that hung on the wall. King Archibald strode over to the tapestry and whipped it aside. This was quite a feat, as the tapestries were all very heavy. The whipping aside of the tapestry wafted a cloud of cheap eau-de-cologne deep into the room, prompting all the windows to be simultaneously thrown open. The windows were then just as simultaneously and promptly slammed shut, because Millicent flew by and blew a huge fireball at the castle.

Prince Colah stood very still with his eyes shut, hoping the King could not see him.

"Colah…" King Archibald said gently, but in a very cold manner.

Prince Colah tried to squeeze his eyes shut even tighter.

"COLAH!" Shouted King Archibald.

Prince Colah's eyes popped opened and he jumped a little, as though he was surprised to see King Archibald standing in front of him.

"Oh, hello?"

"Where is my daughter?"

"Who?"

"The princess, the woman you are going to marry."

"Oh! Her! I dunno where she is. I thought she came in with… with… with…?" Prince Colah acted as though he was trying to see who had been with the princess last.

"Fool."

King Archibald turned away in disgust, and promptly bumped into the Chancellor who had slithered up behind him.

"My liege" he squirmed. "I was just about to send a search party out for you because we were all getting very worried and did not know what had happened to you, so I took it upon myself to get a search part…"

"Have you seen the princess?" King Archibald interrupted.

"Er… um… No?"

"You either have, or you have not, it is very simple."

King Archibald was beginning to think that he was the only one left in the kingdom with any sort of working brain. While not entirely true, it was not too far from the truth. You see, when people become scared, for example, when a large hungry dragon flies overhead, they tend to lose their capacity to think straight, among other things, but we will not talk of that. Well, most people are like that. Some suddenly start thinking very clearly.

King Archibald continued his search for the princess, but it soon became obvious no one had actually taken the time to make sure the bride-to-be, and heir to the throne, was safe. He returned to Prince Colah, who had returned to the safety of the tapestry. King Archibald knew he would regret this conversation, but no one else had expressed any interest in his daughter.

Apart from the little drooling soldier, but he was of no consequence.

King Archibald mused for a fleeting second as to the whereabouts of whatever-his-name-was.

King Archibald decided to rip the tapestry; Prince Colah was hiding behind, from the wall, thus leaving Prince Colah nowhere to hide.

"Cooler," King Archibald said, somewhat resignedly,

"You will go and find my..."

"Er... My name is Colah..."

"That's what I said," said the King glaring at Prince Colah.

Prince Colah opened his mouth as though to say something, but decided against it.

"You are going to go outside and search for the princess...," continued the King.

"Why me?" whined the sniveling Prince.

"Because..." said King Archibald trying very hard not to lose his temper "...you are betrothed to her and it is only..."

"Be... what to her?"

"Betrothed," King Archibald could see the Prince was having a very hard time with the word.

"Betrothed means...why me...?" sighed King Archibald. "Betro..." The king continued.

"Betrothingy, means why me?" interrupted the puzzled prince.

"Be quiet. Betrothed means that you have promised to marry, so it is your duty to go and find her."

"Find who?" Prince Colah said, hoping the king would have forgotten.

Luckily, for Prince Colah, one of the footmen, who had been dragged off to the dungeons, managed to convince the guards he knew the whereabouts of the princess. He also said King Archibald would rather know the whereabouts of the princess, than have the footman thrown into the dungeon. At first, the guard doubted the truth of the footman's statement, but decided it was probably wiser to err on the side of caution. The guard then escorted the footman back to the throne room.

The footman being returned to the throne room was lucky for Prince Colah, because King Archibald was trying to pull Prince Colah's head off. He was almost interrupted by a guard tapping him on the shoulder, then two guards trying to pull their king off the Prince, then five guards. The five guards mostly succeeded. Well, at least they had the king's attention. Well, most of the king's attention.

King Archibald, a tenacious man, still held onto Colah's neck with one hand while the footman explained how he had seen the princess, among others, being carried away in the huge claws of the dragon.

There was a heavy thud and the sound of Prince Colah coughing on the floor. Then there was some shouting and other such commotion as King Archibald tried to rip the footman's head off. Then five more of the guards joined the first five, and tried to prevent their king from ripping the footman's head off.

The footman was somewhat elated to be thrown back into the dungeon, and to be out of the incessant grip of the king. The frogs began protesting the fact that their cell was becoming overcrowded, by increasing the volume and frequency of their croaking.

Prince Gaston was very happy to have someone new to talk with. He was not happy about the noisy frog protest though, nor were the three footmen. The more they protested the frogs' protest, the more the frogs protested. Needless to say, but Prince Gaston was very, very happy to be suddenly let out of the dungeon and given a hot bath (the bath in his cell only had cold water) and clean clothes.

The frogs' protest in regard to the overcrowding was not very effective, so one of the younger and more adventurous frogs decided to try and escape by hopping through the bars of their cell. When the other frogs saw that it was not only possible but also very easy, they all went very quiet for a few seconds.

Everyone went so quiet that it was quite scary.

Then all of a sudden the frogs started up again but not with the protest croaking, this was very different, their obvious excitement filled the air so much even some of their human cellmates were getting excited. Well, until they too tried hopping trough the bars. The frogs were infinitely more successful at getting through the bars, and were soon happily hopping and croaking their way out of the dungeon. The croaking fading further and further away made everyone happy, all that croaking can get on one's nerves.

PRINCE GASTON IS RELEASED.

Freshly bathed, shaved and dressed in clean clothes befitting a prince, Prince Gaston was escorted to the king's private chamber. Inside the chamber, King Archibald was sitting on a very ornately carved, heavy wooden chair, and did not get up when Gaston entered the room. The guards who had escorted Prince Gaston from the dungeons, left as quickly as they could. Just as Prince Gaston was thinking he and the King were alone, the Chancellor stood up from behind the throne.

"My dear Prince Gaston, how good it is to see you again! Did you enjoy your trip?" King Archibald asked, his voice dripping with insincerity.

"My trip? What the… Are you nuts? I have been stuck in your rotten little…"

"Want to go on another trip?" King Archibald asked menacingly.

"Err… It was a lovely trip. Thank you for asking, your Highness."

"Call me Archie." King Archibald said generously.

"You have to be joking. Last time I called you… that, you had me thrown into one of your…"

"No, it's fine. Really, I don't mind. Please."

"Well…ok…Archie…" Prince Gaston said carefully, noticing that Archie's face flushed red but he still smiled… a bit. Prince Gaston thought to himself, Archie must want something very badly. Prince Gaston decided to take full advantage of the situation.

"You know what, Archie, it was an awfully long trip, Archie, and no good food or wine, Archie, not even any fresh fruit, Archie. Archie, do you think that you could arrange for some supper or something? Hmm? Archie?"

King Archibald, barely controlling his temper, appeared to be struggling against a strong desire to leap up from the throne. It was then Prince Gaston realized the thick belt the king was wearing was also binding him to his throne. Prince Gaston decided to tone down his taunting of the king.

"Maybe just a light snack for now?" inquired the prince.

"Why of course, just as soon as we finish our little conversation. I'm sure the kitchen can put a little feast together for you." King Archibald said, at last controlling his displeasure… a bit.

"Yes…" the Chancellor chimed in, "…and after you have feasted you can hel… owwww!"

The reason the Chancellor suddenly said "owwww" was King Archibald had just, rather rudely, shoved his elbow into the Chancellor's leg to shut him up. King Archibald was not quite ready to reveal to Prince Gaston just why he had had him released from the dungeons. He wanted to find out what Prince Gaston's intentions were concerning Princess Maybel. If Prince Gaston had come to Blognasee with the intention of wooing Princess Maybel that would complicate some of King Archibald's plans. If not, then the plan King Archibald was planning would work, if everything went according to plan.

Prince Gaston was beginning to get a more than a little suspicious.

"Err… just what is it you want?" Prince Gaston asked cautiously.

"Want? What do you mean, Prince? I want nothing more than to entertain you after your nice long trip." King Archibald was not being very convincing.

"If you'll pardon the expression, Archie, dragon–poop! You have some sort of…" Prince Gaston stopped talking as he had noticed King Archibald was struggling to undo the thick leather belt.

The Chancellor was trying to stop the king from undoing the thick leather belt and leaping from the throne to attack Prince

Gaston. This was made quite noticeable by the sound of a very heavy ornately carved throne being dragged across the floor.

"If the dragon doesn't kill him, I will," King Archibald hissed at the Chancellor, calming himself, a little, at the thought.

"Yes, Sire. Of course you will, Sire, but the princess... if he saves her from the dragon, you have to give her hand in marriage...," the Chancellor said, obviously struggling to keep the king seated.

"Er... excuse me..." tried the Prince.

He was ignored.

"Fine. He gets to marry her, but then I get to kill him! Right?"

"Er... excuse me..." tried the Prince again.

Again, he was ignored.

"Sire, it is just... well, that is, it is rather more than a little pointless to kill your new son-in-law. Unless of course you want to give those silly anti-monarchists even more..."

"Fine. He gets to marry her, I don't kill him, but I do get to throw him back..."

"I SAID EXCUSE ME!" yelled the Prince.

"WHAT?" yelled the King and the Chancellor, in unison.

"I don't mean to burst your bubble Archie, but what makes you think I want to marry your daughter?" said Prince Gaston starting to move from mere suspicion to annoyance.

"You are a Prince, aren't you?" sneered the king.

"Yes, but I fail to..." Prince Gaston began cautiously.

"And traditionally princes marry princesses..." the king went on, ignoring the prince.

"That may be true but..." Prince Gaston's suspicion was rising again.

"...especially after saving the princess." continued King Archibald ignoring the prince again.

"Well, yes, according to the various fairy ta... Save the princess? Save her from what?" Prince Gaston was now thoroughly suspicious.

"You are not currently married, are you?" piped in the Chancellor.

"No, not surprising since having spent the last couple of years…" began Prince Gaston a tad confused and miffed by the question.

"Oh that's all water over the bridge now." interrupted King Archibald.

"Er, sire that's dam." corrected Frank.

"What? Are you swearing at me?"

"No Sire, I would not even begin to think about the possibility of drea…"

"Shut up Frank. As I was saying Gaston, that's all water over the bridge…?"Frank couldn't help himself.

"Water over the dam, sire, you said over the bridge."

"What?" said King Archibald and Prince Gaston in unison

"Frank, be quiet," said the king quietly.

"As I was saying, that's all water under the bridge now," continued King Archibald, giving Frank a sideways glare.

"Maybe for you but I still fail…" began the prince

"You better not fail, Prince, because if you do your life won't…" the king interjected.

"What, exactly, do you mean by I'd better not fail? Fail to what, exactly?" Prince Gaston asked trying to make sense of the conversation.

"If you fail to rescue my daughter from the dragon!" said the king as though it had been crystal clear all along that that was the generally accepted topic.

"What are you talking about? What dragon?" Prince Gaston could feel the suspicion rising again.

"Where have you been for…?" began the king.

"Sitting in one of your dirty rotten stinking dungeons…"

"Oh, I suppose you're going to keep bringing that up. I don't understand. Why you can't let bygones be bygones?" King Archibald sounded as though his feelings had been horribly hurt by Prince Gaston's description of the dungeons.

"What? No." the prince answered firmly, suspecting the hurt in King Archibald's voice was a ruse.

"I see. So you're too scared then?" taunted King Archibald, trying a different tactic.

"I'm not scared..." started Prince Gaston, somewhat defensively.

"So you'll go after the dragon then?" interrupted the King.

"Are you insane? What makes you think I am going to -much less consider- chase after some dragon that -I'm guessing here- has carried off your precious princess..." Prince Gaston said, thinking that he was finally getting some control of the situation.

"How about I agree not to poke-you-in-the-eye-with-sharp-sticks and slap-you-in-the-face-with-several-wet-fish, right now? We haven't had a good old fashioned eye-poking *and* fish-slapping for a very long time." King Archibald threatened.

"Ooh... now I'm really scared," mocked the prince.

"Well, then, maybe a few more years in the dungeon with the frogs will get your attention," the king stated in a most matter-of-fact way.

Without batting an eye, Prince Gaston asked,

"And just where, does this dragon live?"

The next few hours were spent getting Prince Gaston ready, which included finding new armor, some food, a horse, and some weapons. King Archibald resisted giving Prince Gaston any weapons until it was explained, several times, the prince probably stood a better chance of rescuing the princess if he had something with which to fight and hopefully dispose of the dragon. Again, Prince Gaston asked the question that was a little hard to answer.

"Just where does this dragon of yours live anyway?"

"It's not my dragon," answered King Archibald.

"I didn't think..." started Prince Gaston.

"That's the trouble with you young people, you just don't think."

"That's not what I meant."

"Do you really think I would let my darling daughter be carried off by my own dragon?"

"Well, no but... You have your own dragon?"

"No, but if I did I wouldn't." explained King Archibald.

"What? Oh, never mind. Does anyone know where I can find the dragon?" the Prince asked again.

Inquiries were made and it soon became apparent that, as nobody had actually been to where the dragons were rumored to live, and returned, nobody was even sure the dragons did live there or exactly how to get there, wherever it was.

Then Johnson, the soldier who had climbed the tower to ask Kevin what all the fuss was about when Prince Colah had shown up, and had tried relaying the messages from Kevin regarding the burning farmhouse, began to regret what he was about to suggest.

"Er... Sire, I think Kev... Er... the Sergeant-of-the-Tall-Tower..." Luckily, for Johnson, he remembered Kevin's name was still not to be mentioned anywhere close to the castle let alone the king.

"Who? What? Captain?" spluttered the king.

"Sire." The Captain-of-the-guard clicked his heels together and saluted sharply.

"Captain, I think this soldier is actually trying to speak directly to me, which is intolerable. Throw him in the dungeon, and then have him boiled in fish oil, or something."

"Yes,...Sire." The Captain turned to two other soldiers who were standing inattentively nearby. They looked up nonchalantly when the Captain spoke.

"Throw him into the dungeon," the Captain ordered.

"Who?"

"What?" the Captain asked incredulously.

"Whom do you want us to throw in the dungeon?" the taller of the two asked.

"Johnson." answered the Captain.

"Why?" the shorter of the two asked.

"Yeah, what'd he do?" added the taller.

"Lieutenant!" the Captain called.

The Lieutenant wandered into the stable where the king, the Chancellor, a couple of royal family members dressed as generals (even though they really had nothing at all to do with the day to day running of the King's Guard) and Prince Gaston, were gathered around a table covered with maps. By this time, King Archibald and the others who had been pondering the maps stopped what they were doing to watch.

King Archibald could hardly believe what he was witnessing. The Chancellor was hoping no one would bring up the subject of the low pay the guards were actually getting, because he was pocketing the raise that King Archibald had authorized several months ago. The generals were trying to hide behind Prince Gaston, because they did not want to get involved. Prince Gaston began re-considering the quality of the weapons he had been given, as it seemed almost everyone in the kingdom of Blognasee could not care less about the tasks they were set. He was also thinking the horse he was to ride was probably one of the more intelligent creatures in the entire kingdom.

The Captain-of-the-Guard was hoping a hole of just the right size for him to disappear into would suddenly appear in the ground below him, or anywhere, he really did not care where.

A hole did appear but it missed the Captain by several miles and a very surprised cow fell into it. The very surprised cow was even more surprised to be ejected from the hole just before it snapped shut, having realized that it was in the wrong place.

The Lieutenant looked at the Captain-of-the-Guard and wondered why he kept looking at the ground below and all around him as though he was expecting something to appear suddenly.

"Was there something you wanted? Sir?" The Lieutenant added the 'sir' with a reluctant tone. He was still a little miffed at being passed over when the original Captain-of-the-Guard had had to retire. He still felt the job should have gone to him.

"Captain…" King Archibald hissed, "…if you do not carry out my instructions you can throw yourself into the dungeon."

The Captain-of-the-Guard turned a whiter shade of pale than he already had been.

"Lieutenant, escort these three ex-soldiers to the dungeon NOW!" the Captain-of-the-Guard yelled. He yelled because he wanted the Lieutenant to be startled into action instead of looking at the ground and elsewhere, as though he too was hoping a hole for him to jump into would appear. The Captain-of-the-guard was ready to fight for the hole, if it ever decided to appear.

In case you were wondering, the hole never appeared as it was too embarrassed by its earlier mistaken appearance.

The Lieutenant was startled into action and started to push the three soldiers out of the stables. The three soldiers began whining and kept on whining all the way to the dungeon. When the little band got to the dungeons, and were thrown into one of the cells, they stopped whining. The cell was well furnished; it even had a bath. It was much better than the barrack–room, where they had to share a bucket with twenty other soldiers. Moreover, even better yet, there were three footmen. Somewhat surly footmen, but they were footmen nonetheless. The only bad things about the cell were a large cast iron object that looked something like a bell that had fallen a great distance, which took up a fair amount of space, and there were now six occupants. Mind you, as someone had cut a doorway into the bell to gain access to the bath, it did provide a degree of privacy to anyone using the bath. No one cared that the frogs were no longer occupying the dungeon. It was in fact quite peaceful in the dungeons now, no one barking orders at them, none of the clamor of life in the barracks and no croaking frogs.

As the cell door was slammed shut behind them, Johnson remembered he had had something important to tell the King.

"Do you think I should remind King Archie about Kevin?" Johnson asked the Lieutenant.

"Who?" the Lieutenant asked.

"Kevin? Plane? The Sergeant-of-the-Tall-Tower?"

"Oh. Him. I could have you thrown in the dungeon for mentioning his name."

"Look around you."

"Oh. Yeah. Silly of me. What about him?"

"Well, he did see the dragon a couple of days ago and he did try to warn everybody."

"Yeah, and typical of management, they ignored him." chimed in the taller of the two other guards who just happened to be named Schorter.

"Just wait till the union hears about this." threatened the shorter of the other two guards, whose name coincidentally was Toller.

"Union? What union?" asked the Lieutenant.

"The A.U.P.C.G." said Toller, the shorter of the two.

"The what?" the Lieutenant asked incredulously.

"The Amalgamated Union of Palace and Castle Guards," said Schorter the taller of the two.

"What? Wait a minute, there isn't any such union," the Lieutenant said.

"Yes there is."

"No there isn't."

"Is."

"Not."

"Uhuh."

"Nuhuh"

This exchange went on for a while until finally:

"Will you three shut up?" cried an exasperated Johnson. "There is no such union and I have…"

"Spoilsport!" the taller guard, Schorter, sneered.

"See, I knew it!" retorted the Lieutenant.

"Had you going, though," the shorter guard, Toller, taunted.

"Did not."

"Did."

"Not."

"Did."

"Shut up!" yelled Johnson. "You're worse than a couple of kids."

"Go on, admit it. You were falling for it, weren't you?" Schorter scoffed at the Lieutenant.

"Shut the heck up! And I wasn't. I knew you were trying to pull my leg." yelled the Lieutenant, not exactly sure of himself. He actually yelled something much ruder, but it would not be nice of me to repeat it.

"Er… when you have quite finished, I still have some important information for the king and Prince Gaston," tried Johnson.

"Well if it's so important, why didn't you tell him yourself?" asked the Lieutenant.

"I tried to, remember? That's why we're down here now. "

"Oh, right. Tell you what, you tell me your 'important information' and I'll pass it on to the Captain-of-the-Guard and he can…"

"If we had a union…" started Schorter.

"If you don't shut up I'll have you…"

"You'll have us what? Sent to the dungeons?" Toller teased.

"No. I'll have you promoted to the highest position…"

"We're shutting up!" Toller and Schorter said, making sewing motions over their lips. Along with cars, zippers were a long way off from being invented.

The Lieutenant asked Johnson what it was he was going to tell the King. Johnson again explained about Kevin seeing the dragon.

"Kevin therefore must have seen where it had come from or gone to." Johnson concluded.

"Well, you wait here and I'll see if they want to listen to you. I'll be back in a minute. Really. I will," said the Lieutenant.

Johnson settled down to wait while the Lieutenant left to deliver his message.

"You know the union rep' won't like this," Schorter tried.

"Shut up," Johnson answered

"Management lackey." Toller sneered.

Upon arriving back at the stable, the Lieutenant found King Archibald, Prince Gaston, the Chancellor and the Captain-of-the-Guard still going over the maps. The generals had fallen asleep on some bales of hay.

"Sire," the Lieutenant said nervously.

"Yes, what is it?" snapped the King impatiently.

"Er… I er…"

"Either speak or join the others in the dungeon"

"Well Sire, I was thinking…"

"Did you hurt yourself?" asked King Archibald.

"Beg pardon, Sire?" asked the Lieutenant bewildered.

"What was it you were straining you brain over?"

"Well, Sire, I was thinking…"

"Makes a nice change."

"…that maybe Kev… er… I mean the Sergeant-of-the-Tall-Tower must have seen where the dragon came from and could probably…"

"Don't be preposterous," said King Archibald, turning to the Captain-of-the-Guard.

"Captain, I've just had a brilliant idea. Bring the Sergeant-of-the-Tall-Tower here. I have a feeling that he may have seen where the dragon went."

"Yes Sire, but you…" started the Captain.

"Just bring him here."

"But Sire, you gave strict orders that he was never to leave the tower," whined the Captain.

"Stop whining and bring him here! Not that I should have to remind you, but I am your king, and as such I can change my mind if I feel like doing so. Why are you still standing there?" asked King Archibald.

The Lieutenant was beginning to think that a union was not such bad idea.

A few hours later Johnson was thinking the same, as no one had come to release him from the cell for having had such a brilliant idea.

The Captain-of-the-Guard shuffled out of the stable muttering to himself about how he never wanted the job of Captain-of-the-Guard and that he was quite happy, as the head dishwasher, before his meddling mother stuck her nose in his affairs. Outside the stable, he found two soldiers sitting on the ground drinking from an earthenware jug filled with a rose-scented liquid. The Captain-of-the-Guard called them over to him.

A short while later he walked over to them. They slowly

looked up and with much grunting, groaning and muttering about being disturbed on their break by a dishwasher, stood up and sort of saluted. The Captain-of-the-Guard told them to go to the Tall Tower and bring Kevin back to the stables. They looked blankly at him so he repeated his orders, and when it finally sunk in the soldiers sauntered off in the general direction of the Tall Tower.

When they got there, they looked up at the Tall Tower and saw the top was missing and someone had apparently dumped a pile of rubble in its place. Poking out of the top of the pile of rubble was a bright shiny bell. The soldiers looked at each other, turned around, and went unhurriedly back to the stables.

The Captain-of-the-Guard was waiting outside the stables, crouching on the ground and hopping about like some demented frog. I think the stress of his job was getting to him. When he realized the soldiers had returned, the Captain-of-the-Guard stood up and brushed himself off as though nothing out of the ordinary was going on.

"Well, where is he?" the Captain-of-the-Guard demanded, trying to appear as though hopping around like a demented frog was quite normal behavior.

"Why were you hopping about like a demented frog?" asked the older of the two soldiers.

"I wasn't. Where is he?" the Captain-of-the-Guard demanded again.

"Yes you were." the elder of the soldiers answered.

"Where's who?" asked the younger of the two soldiers.

"No I was not. The Sergeant-of-the-Tall-Tower." snapped the Captain-of-the-Guard.

"Yes you were!" exclaimed the elder soldier.

"He's probably in the Tall-Tower." said the younger soldier whose name happened to be Elldar.

"It doesn't matter. I know that..." the Captain-of-the-Guard was losing his patience and beginning to get confused by trying to hold two conversations at once.

"Why'd you ask where he was then?" said Elldar.

"I think it does matter, when a senior officer starts hopping abou…" began the elder of the two.

"Just forget it, will you! Because I sent you to the Tall-Tower to bring the Sergeant-of-the-Tall-Tower here." explained the Captain-of-the-Guard. His face was beginning to turn red with anger, and embarrassment.

"Is it some sort of exercise routine?" asked the elder of the two soldiers whose name just happened to be Yungor.

"It's gone." said Elldar.

"What? No! What's gone?" the Captain-of-the-Guard asked his voice almost cracking with hysteria.

"The top of the tower," said Elldar, the younger of the two soldiers.

"Were you trying to communicate with the frogs?" inquired Yungor.

"Will you shut up? What are you talking about?"

"Remember the Tall Tower? It used to have a thingy on top of it," said Yungor, the elder of the two.

"A 'thingy.' What in the world is a 'thingy'?" asked the Captain-of-the-Guard, trying not to lose his mind.

"So what, then?" asked Yungor

"You know. The thingy. That had the bell in it," said Elldar the younger.

"Do you mean the belfry?" the Captain-of-the-Guard tried.

"Oh so you're ignoring me now" said Yungor the elder, sounding hurt.

"What about it?" asked the Captain-of-the-Guard.

"What about what?" asked Elldar.

"THE BELFRY!!" yelled the Captain-of-the-Guard.

"Well, if you're going to ignore me and yell at us, we're not going to tell you," said Yungor.

"That's right. The union rulebook, states quite clearly that you are not allowed to yell at us…" agreed Elldar.

"…or ignore us…" put in Yungor.

"…and if you do, we have the right to…"

"Union? What union?" The Captain-of-the-Guard was feeling

like he could quite happily hop around like a demented frog for the rest of his life. He resisted the urge.

It was at that exact moment the Lieutenant stepped inelegantly out of the stables. Well, he did not exactly "step inelegantly" as much as land on his feet, due to the King throwing him out of the stables. The King was getting more than a little impatient waiting for the Sergeant-of-the-Tall-Tower to arrive, and had decided the Lieutenant should go and assist the Captain-of-the-Guard in his endeavors.

"Don't tell me, the A.U.P.C.G., which does not…" the Lieutenant said stumbling to a standstill next to the others.

"The what?" Asked the others in unison.

"The Amalgamated Union of Palace and Castle Guards. But it's a…" said the Lieutenant trying to explain.

"Never heard of it," said Elldar.

"I'm sure you haven't, Toller and Schorter tried to…" started the Lieutenant.

"Those fools don't know anything." interrupted Yungor the elder guard.

"Yeah we belong to the P.C.G.U.U.W.," said Elldar the younger guard.

"Local 687," added Yungor.

"Before I promote you to the highest position in the Kingdom, tell me what you are talking about, and why you did not bring the Sergeant-of-the-Tall-Tower back here with you?" the Captain-of-the-Guard asked, barely controlling his emotions and knowing that he was not going to like the answer.

"The P.C.G.U.U.W.? It's the Palace and Castle Guards Union of United Workers, and the reason we did not bring The Sergeant-of-the-Tall-Tower back with us is that the thingy…"

"Belfry," reminded the Captain-of-the-Guard.

"…belfry has been demolished."

The Captain-of-the-Guard, in as controlled a voice as he could muster, told the Lieutenant to take Yungor and Elldar and whoever else might be needed to the top of the tower, and find out exactly what had happened to the Sergeant-of-the-Tall-Tower.

Then he instructed them to bring the Sergeant-of-the-Tall-Tower back to the stables or report directly to the king as to why they had failed to do so. As none of them wanted to come even close to the king in his present state of mind, the three ran as fast as they could to find out what had happened to Kevin.

When everybody had left, the Captain-of-the-Guard reached up to the sky and cried. "Why me? What does it mean?"

"Betrothed?" queried a voice behind him.

The Captain-of-the-Guard turned to see Prince Colah trying to sneak out of the castle.

KEVIN MEETS THE KING.

Exactly what had happened to Kevin was, when Millicent's tail had smashed into the belfry and the belfry began to collapse on top of him, Kevin dove for cover under his bed that he had luckily placed over the trap door. However, now the trap door was under Kevin and he was under the bed and the bed was under the rubble that was once the belfry, mixed in with several hundred books, and the major part of the rubble was under the new bell. Kevin was unable to move, let alone open the trap door, which was still locked from the other side. The floor was beginning to make creaking noises in protest of all the extra weight it was being asked to bear.

Kevin started imagining that he was going to return to the dungeons via the same route he had taken a couple of years ago.

Kevin cried.

Kevin stopped crying.

Kevin stopped crying because he heard voices directly below him. The voices Kevin heard were those of the rescue team (*I use the term team loosely*) of soldiers and villagers who had been coerced into helping extract Kevin from the rubble that was once the belfry.

"Owwwwwww!!!" cried Kevin.

Kevin cried "Owwwwwww!!!" because somebody had shoved something very sharp through the closed trap door and had managed to injure Kevin. Slightly, but it still hurt.

The reason something sharp had been shoved through the closed trap door was, eighteen people had gathered at the top of the narrow staircase.

Those of you who have had a personal experience of eighteen people in a very confined space will understand why it is not a good idea at any time. If you have not had an experience like that, consider yourself lucky. In this situation, it was made worse, as each of the eighteen people were trying to tell the other seventeen what to do. It is safe to say the atmosphere at the top of the Tall-Tower, just below the trap door, was fraught-with anger and a few other emotions. Things were not helped by the fact that they had forgotten to bring the key for the lock on the trapdoor.

Anyway, the sharp object, which had been thrust through the trap door, was a lance someone had brought with them "just in case the dragon is hiding up there."

The owner of the lance had been the target of much derision, and in protest, gestured rather forcibly with the lance, thrusting the point through the closed trap door, slightly injuring Kevin. The good part of the incident was that it shut everybody up.

"Owwwwwww!!!" cried Kevin.

That is when everybody shut up.

"Well, at least he's still alive," Sumbuddy, one of the soldiers, said.

"What was your first clue?" Ells, one of the villagers asked, rather sarcastically.

"Don't start with me," Sumbuddy snapped.

The whole crowd started yelling and pushing again. Finally, Esau-the-carpenter told everyone to go back downstairs while he and Prentice, Esau's trainee/assistant, took the trap door apart, after removing the lance. The actual time it took to release the trap door was about a minute. Esau, though, still charged his normal minimum of four hours and added another two hundred percent for priority charges plus overtime for Prentice, who incidentally saw not a pentso, or even a qgtdgt of the overtime pay. Once the two pins for the hinges on the trap door were pulled out and the door itself removed, a sobbing Kevin fell out head first from his prison.

The three then had to run down the stairs, as the bed that

was on top of Kevin, and under several hundred books and all the rubble that was once a nice new belfry, gave way and came through the hole made by the floor. The floor made the hole because it did not want to hold all the extra weight anymore. The new bell followed all of the rubble, which was once a nice new belfry, and several hundred books.

When Kevin, Esau, and Prentice emerged from the drab doorway at the bottom of the tower, they were closely followed by a ringing cloud of dust, rubble, and bits of paper. The ringing stopped abruptly when the bell crashed into the small but drab doorway.

The rest of the "rescue team" seized Kevin and dragged him off to the stables. When they arrived, the team found the Captain-of-the-Guard on his knees, banging his head on the ground. After a few seconds, the Captain-of-the-Guard realized he was not alone. He stopped banging his head on the ground, pretended to look for something very small, find it and place it in his pocket. Then he pretended to notice the small crowd surrounding him, and stood up. He was able to fool not one of them.

"Jolly good. Thank you. Sergeant-of-the-Tall-Tower step forward, and prepare to meet your king." The Captain-of-the-Guard said, trying to act nonchalantly. Still not fooling anyone.

Kevin stepped forward. He was covered in dust, bits of rubble and even had a couple of pages from a book or two, tangled in his hair, which he tried to brush off.

"Never mind that." The Captain-of-the-Guard snapped as he took Kevin by the arm.

"Owwwww." Cried Kevin.

The Captain-of-the-Guard had grabbed Kevin's injured arm.

"Sorry." Said the Captain-of-the-Guard and grabbed Kevin's other arm.

The Captain-of-the-Guard led Kevin into the stable, where King Archibald, Prince Gaston, and the Chancellor were sitting around the map table. The map table now had the remains of a feast fit for a king, fittingly enough, laid out on it. The generals having feasted were once again curled up in one of the stalls snoring away. The king looked up. Kevin looked hungrily at the feast and started drooling.

"Ah, Captain, at last. I was becoming so worried about you." There was more than a tinge of sarcasm in King Archibald's voice.

"This must be our Sergeant-of-the-Tall-Tower. Come in. Come in, don't be shy." The King said waving them over to the table. Kevin and the Captain-of-the-Guard inched over to stand in front of the table.

"What's your name?" King Archibald asked.

"Kevin." Answered Kevin

"Just plain Kevin, eh? There was a lad in the village called Kevin Plane. Used to get into all sorts of trouble, but that can't be you, can it?" The King asked innocently.

"Yesoww." Kevin replied.

Kevin replied 'Yesoww' because the Captain-of-the-Guard's grip on Kevin's uninjured arm suddenly became very painful.

"You know, I thought it was you. I remember you drooled at the Princess once. Would you like to see her again?" asked the King without the slightest hint of sincerity.

"I would like nothing more Sire, for she is the true love..."

"Right. I'm sure that's very nice but you should know she is going to marry Prince Gaston here," sneered the King, waving a hand in Gaston's direction.

Kevin started to say something, but stopped when he saw Prince Gaston's face.

"But there'll be plenty of time for all of that later. First you are going to show Gaston how to find the dragon, and assist him in rescuing my precious princess."

The King turned back to the maps, totally ignoring the puzzled expression on the faces of Kevin and Prince Gaston, in fact, everyone was looking very puzzled.

While he had been waiting, King Archibald had had plenty of time to think about a few things. What he had been thinking about was that he might be able to kill two birds with one stone.

For the more sensitive of you, I want to let you know the king was not actually thinking of killing any birds, really. It is just an expression, so please do not worry any more about any birds being killed.

King Archibald had decided he would be able to solve a couple of problems by sending Kevin and Prince Gaston off to rescue his daughter. First, they might actually succeed and free the princess; and second, in the process, they might be mortally wounded, and he would be rid of them. On the other hand, if they all made it back, King Archibald had no doubt that Maybel would want to marry Gaston rather than Kevin. Gaston was, after all, a real Prince and far more handsome than Kevin. That would solve the problem of Kevin, who would undoubtedly leave the Kingdom in shame. The King though, did not intend to let Prince Gaston marry his daughter, as he did not want a son-in-law he could not control. Prince Colah might be a cowardly weasel, but at least he was a controllable cowardly weasel. The King knew once Kevin was gone, thinking Gaston and Maybel were in love and to be married, he could then find a way of getting rid of Gaston and thereby leave Prince Colah as the only person eligible to marry his daughter.

What the King did not know, however, will become quite clear to you as you read on.

Kevin was asked if he had seen the dragon's lair, or at least knew where it was. Kevin stated he had a very good idea, and felt quite capable of guiding the prince. The others in the stable felt very differently as they thought Kevin, if you will pardon the expression, would have a hard time finding his own rear end on a sunny day.

What they did not know will also be revealed as you read on.

The preparations for the expedition were finalized, and Prince Gaston and Kevin left the castle a few hours later, into the dark night. A small crowd gathered to wish them well on their sojourn. The small crowd did not stop waving and offering encouraging tips on how to find and slay the dragon until

Gaston and Kevin had reached the other end of the drawbridge. The drawbridge was promptly raised the very second Kevin and Prince Gaston had stepped off it. Prince Gaston and Kevin ignored the surprised cries and two splashes that came from the moat. They did not see the young couple, once again, try scrambling out of the thick mud, they did hear the girl slap the boy, and vow never to go on a date with him again.

As the small crowd, within the castle walls, turned away and headed to their nice cozy beds, it was possible to hear the majority of them saying things like "Fool's errand" and "Well, that's the last we'll see of them."

KEVIN'S QUEST BEGINS.

Once Prince Gaston and Kevin had rounded a bend in the road to the village, Prince Gaston looked over his shoulder towards the castle, and saw that all the lights in the castle windows had gone out. When he was quite certain no one was watching them, he leaned down from his horse and spoke to Kevin.

"Kevin, I like you a lot, and I really did enjoy our conversations in the dungeon, but I am out of here!"

Kevin looked up at the Prince. Kevin had not been given a horse, or rather, he had, but he kept falling off, so it was decided he would be better off on foot. As he was still very nervous around animals and he could out run most of the horses in the kingdom anyway, he was quite happy to be on foot.

"What do you mean you're 'out of here'?" he asked.

"Exactly what I said. If your king thinks I am going to rescue his daughter and bring her back so I can marry her, then he's out of his tiny mind. I was only passing through, this grotty little Kingdom, when my horse went lame. I stopped at the castle to see if I could trade him in for a new one. That was my second mistake. Then I made my third mistake and called Archie, Archie."

"Your third mistake? What was your first mistake then?" Kevin inquired.

"My first mistake was buying a cheap map from a merchant who was wearing a rather nice crown. Looked a lot like Archie's but was obviously the genuine article," Prince Gaston replied.

"Oh," said Kevin

"If you'll take my advice, you'll come with me back to Arabacca, my father, King Ventea's, country, and leave this dump."

"I can't do that. What about Princess Maybel?"

"Forget about her. She won't want to have anything to do with you. Anyway, she's probably dragon food by now."

"I can't. I love her and she loves me. And I know she's still alive."

"What do you mean? You don't really know her! The first time you met, you drooled at her, and she yelled at you. She even threatened to have you tortured! And when you were in the dungeon, all you had were a few brief encounters, until Archie put a stop to all of that."

"That first meeting was a long time ago and she was only re-acting to the stress of the moment and she told me the drooling was what attracted her to me in the first place. Those 'few brief encounters' were all we needed…" Kevin said, somewhat defen-sively.

"Oh come on, that was hardly enough time to get to know her. It's not like we're living one of those 'Fantastical Tales' stories." Prince Gaston scoffed.

The Fantastical Tales series of comic books was the most popular form of storytelling since the days of the Tell-Ins. They also had advertisements for all sorts of "magical and wondrous" goodies. Most of which were a great disappointment to those that sent off their hard earned pentsos.

"It was enough time for us to realize that we are meant for each other." Kevin countered.

"Even so, do you really think good old Archie will let you marry his precious little princess?" Prince Gaston interrupted.

"Well, if you're not going to help me rescue her, I stand a better chance," replied Kevin with a confident tone in his voice.

"But you're not a prince! There's no way Archie will allow you to marry Maybel!" Prince Gaston pointed out.

"Ah, well, you see I don't have to be a prince! In fact the dragon is probably the best thing that could have happened to us," Kevin said very sincerely.

"What are you talking about?" Prince Gaston sounded con-fused.

"Well, when I was on duty in the Tall Tower, I read a lot of books." Kevin explained.

"So?"

"One of the books was the Rules and Regulations of The Kingdom of Blognasee, and rule number 47,630,958 part H, clearly states whomsoever rescues the Princess is entitled to ask for her hand in marriage. As she and I are so deeply in love she will not refuse my request, so Archie will have to let us be married." Kevin said confidently.

"I bet there's some sort of loop-hole letting Archie out of that one," Prince Gaston said knowingly.

"I read the book cover to cover. I couldn't find one." Kevin said matter-of-factly.

"Was it the latest edition? You know Archie's very sneaky."

"Of course."

"Oh... Well, I wish you good luck then. Here, take this sword; I won't need it where I'm going." Gaston unbuckled his belt, slid the scabbard -with the sword in it- off, and handed it to Kevin.

"I would give you the horse, but you don't need it as much as I, I need to get away from here as fast as I can. Good-bye Kevin and I hope it all works out for you." Prince Gaston turned his horse and galloped away.

"Good bye then." Kevin said to the cloud of dust the horse was kicking up.

"Bye. Let me know how it all works out!" called the Prince.

"Thanks for the sword!" Kevin shouted to the rapidly fading sound of horse hooves pounding the ground.

Kevin stood still and watched, as the dust cloud faded into the night. Kevin turned toward the village and went to the Big Bore Inn and, much to the surprise of the patrons and Kevin's parents he did not bump into anyone, knock over any tables or spill anything. What Kevin did do, was go up to his old room and collect a few items he felt he might need on his journey. When he came back down to the bar, Kevin stopped and spent a few minutes letting his parents know what he was going to do and to not worry about him. Barry and Martha, like most of the patrons, kept their eyes glued to the sword dangling at Kevin's side fearing that somehow Kevin was going to injure either himself, or worse yet, one of them.

After Kevin had finished sharing his plans, he waited a few seconds for them to react. He eventually took their frightened stares to mean they were too scared for him to speak, so he calmly shook his father's hand, gave his mother a hug and walked out into the night.

A few seconds after the door closed behind Kevin, everyone turned to one another and asked what Kevin had said, they were all too busy worrying about the sword to listen to him. Kevin's mother said that she thought she heard him say something about rescuing Princess Maybel from a dragon and then marrying her.

"Only my s ...Kevin... would go off, rescue a princess from a dragon and then marry the dragon! What if it's not a girl dragon?" Barry exclaimed throwing his hands up in the air.

"Are you sure his ours?" Barry asked Martha, for the twenty-nine thousandth time.

Martha rolled her eyes and walked away from him, muttering "He's yours alright".

The crowd in the bar all roared with laughter.

Kevin paused for a minute outside the door of the Big Bore. Just as he stepped away to begin his journey he heard a huge roar of laughter erupt from inside. Kevin stopped, looked back at the door of the tavern, shrugged, and then, once again, checked the contents of the leather satchel he had slung over his shoulder. Kevin turned his face up to the stars, looked around and strode off in the direction of the Dark and Scary Forest and the mountains. Kevin had not looked at the stars whimsically; he had taken note of their position in the sky relative to the moon that hung like a great mottled pearl over Paassda.

Another of the books Kevin had been reading in the top of the Tall Tower was about navigating by using the stars.

After a few hours, Kevin grew tired, and found a cozy little place to curl up and go to sleep.

The next morning Kevin awoke and sat up. He immediately regretted doing so because he had fallen asleep under a very prickly variety of rose bush. As he picked the thorns out of his hair and other places, he looked around and got his bearings. Instead of using the stars, he used the sun and his shadow. Kevin ate a few of the roses. One of the many books Kevin had read was a very detailed, albeit unscientific, study of roses and their potential uses, written by a certain Hyacinth McThornbush. According to Hyacinth, these particular roses, while thorny, were very tasty and full of good nutrients. After his breakfast, Kevin strapped on the sword Prince Gaston had given him. He picked up his satchel, which had been used as a rather lumpy pillow, and strode off in the direction of the mountains and the Dark and Scary Forest.

THE DARK AND SCARY FOREST.

Kevin reached the edge of the Dark and Scary Forest and stopped. He then turned to his right and ran as fast he could. When he reached the base of the mountains, he was faced with a wall of rock that would not permit any further progress. Kevin ran back to the spot he had started from and kept going. Eventually he reached another massive wall of rock. Kevin sighed and resigned himself to having to go into the Dark and Scary Forest, instead of around it as he had hoped.

One of the books he had read while in the tall tower was a compendium of tales detailing the monsters of the Dark and Scary Forest. What the book had not contained was any details on how to deal with the monsters of the Dark and Scary Forest.

Kevin was, to say the least, very worried. So far, all of the information he had gathered from all the books he had read turned out to be very helpful and equally accurate. He therefore had no reason to doubt the contents of "The Monsters of the Dark and Scary Forest." By Chip Munk, illustrated by W.R.T. Towed.

Kevin simply stood and stared at the mass of trees in front of him. Every now and then he cocked his head to one side as though listening. Kevin's mind was racing thinking about the dangers of the forest and what it would feel like to rescue the princess. He also considered what it would be like if he did not rescue the princess. Prince Gaston's parting words echoed in his head which led to a conversation with himself.

"You know Archie will find a way to not let you marry her..."

"But he will have to, it's the law"

"Really, you think Archie hasn't thought of that already?"

"But I love her and you and I know that love conquers all."

"Ok then go ahead step into the scary forest if you believe that."

"What about the monsters?"

"What about them?"

"They'll eat me."

"So go home then"

"But I have to rescue Maybel"

"So go ahead and step into the forest"

"What about the monsters"

After a couple of hours of going back and forth with his desire to rescue his true love and his un-abiding fears, Kevin made a decision.

With great trepidation, Kevin stepped into the Dark and Scary Forest. After only a few steps, he realized why it was called the Dark and Scary Forest. It was very dark and scary. The reason it was dark was the trees grew very close to each other and the canopy of leaves blocked out almost all of the daylight. The reason it was scary was ...well, dark places tend to be scary.

To make any progress Kevin had to keep walking around huge tree trunks so that his sense of direction soon got confuddled. After a while, Kevin pulled a small device from his satchel that made him feel a little better, it was a small compass. At least he had an idea of the direction he was going but the compass did not make him feel any better about the monsters he could feel lurking in the shadows of the trees.

The monsters lurking in the shadows of the trees watched as Kevin wandered deeper into the dark forest. Some of the monsters licked their lips others drooled hungrily. It had been a very long time since a lone human had wandered into their forest.

Each time Kevin looked around, he kept thinking he had seen the glint of a pair of eyes peering from the darkness. Kevin began to walk faster. Along with the eyes, Kevin also thought he could hear the footfalls of the monsters as they followed him. Every now and then, a sharp snapping sound would reach his ears. Sometimes the sharp snapping sound seemed to be followed by a muffled growl or two.

The monsters following Kevin tried to keep as quiet as possible but some of the larger ones had a hard time not stepping on the dry twigs on the forest floor. The resulting sharp snap of the twig breaking would make them all stop in their tracks. A few of the other monsters would then growl, quietly, at the one who stepped on the twig.

Kevin stopped in his tracks every time he thought he heard a twig snap and looked around him. The darkness of the Dark and Scary Forest hid the monsters very well especially when they stood still, so Kevin, after a few seconds kept moving. He did not feel any the less scared but he knew he was the only one who could rescue his true love, the Princess Maybel, so he forced his urge to run away as fast as he had ever run away before, to a very deep corner of his mind where he could only feel it slightly.

Kevin rounded the base of a huge tree and stepped into a small clearing. He looked up to see an orange-red sky. The sun was setting. Within a few minutes, the sky began to turn purple and then a deep dark blue, a few stars pierced the blue and grew brighter as the sky grew darker. Kevin decided that this was probably as good a place as any to stay the night. Not that it made much difference to being among the trees but what little light there was from the, now, thousands of stars and the moon, helped. The clearing would also give him a chance to see any monsters that might try attacking him.

Kevin walked around the edge of the clearing gathering some dry leaves and fallen branches to make a fire. Suddenly he became very excited, he had found something he had almost given up on ever finding. Around the edge of the clearing were small rose bushes. These roses were indeed quite small compared to most roses but the flowers were exceptional and Kevin recognized them right away. The petals were all the colors of fire and the leaves had a very unique shape, a little bit like a fat arrowhead with sharp spikes around the edges. As the sky grew darker, the flowers seemed to glow brighter as though they were trying to light the deep darkness of the forest. Kevin picked one of the brilliantly colored flowers and ate it. He almost spat it out, it tasted so bad, a minute or so later, he noticed a strange sensation that got him as excited as when he first found them. Kevin quickly gathered more of the roses and stuffed them in his satchel. Soon he had picked all of the roses, Kevin then realized that the forest had grown even darker beyond the clearing, every now and then he thought he heard a rustling in the dry undergrowth as though there were strange creatures creeping around.

The monsters were getting closer.

Kevin quickly collected more firewood and built a large fire in the middle of the clearing. He used a couple of pieces of flint (a type of stone, that when knocked sharply against each other will create sparks) to light the fire. Once the fire was blazing away, Kevin opened up his satchel and pulled out a thin blanket, which he unfolded and spread on the ground. Then he brought out what looked like a large napkin wrapped around something. The something was a large piece of bread and a small wheel of cheese. Kevin tore off a chunk of bread and cheese, took a few of the tiny roses, and made a sandwich. The cheese, while good and strong, did little to mask the taste of the roses, but if he was right, it would be worth suffering a bad taste for a few minutes.

Along with his meal, the firelight helped Kevin feel a bit less scared the warmth of the flames helped too. The drawback was more than ever it seemed like a thousand pairs of eyes were watching him from just beyond the edge of the firelight. Every time he thought he saw a pair of eyes glowing in the dark, out of the corner of his eyes and looked in that direction, the eyes blinked out of sight. He kept trying to tell himself that it was just his imagination.

Of course, you and I know that it was not just his imagination. There really were, a couple of thousand eyes watching him. As soon as he looked in the direction of one of the owners of the eyes, the owner would close them.

As the monsters watched Kevin watching, or rather trying to watch, them they grew hungrier. Some of them even snapped at each other and if the snappee was not quick enough …well I am sure you get the picture… let us just say that the snapper was not so hungry anymore.

Every now and then Kevin heard what sounded like teeth being snapped together and then there were the odd short-lived yelps, followed by wet crunching, munching noises. The noises did not help Kevin feel any less scared, if anything he grew even more frightened. Kevin struggled to stay awake. One of the bits of information in the "Monsters of the Dark and Scary Forest" was that if one found oneself having to spend the night in the Dark and Scary Forest one should not, under any circumstances, fall asleep. The book's author, though, had failed to explain exactly why that was. He may have felt it unnecessary to do so. Kevin's eyes grew itchy and when he tried to blink away the sensation, he realized that his chin had drooped down to his chest.

He had momentarily fallen asleep.

He woke up suddenly, stood up and spun around trying to see beyond the firelight. Soon he sat back down next to the fire and again struggled to stay awake. This scenario was repeated several times.

Each time Kevin's chin sank to his chest the monsters stepped a little closer.

Each time Kevin's chin sank to his chest he would snap his eyes open and look around.

Each time Kevin snapped his eyes open and looked around, the monsters took a step back into the darkness of the trees.

Each time this happened, a few of the monsters gave up and went off to look for some easier prey.

Only the more determined monsters stayed.

Kevin eventually lost his fight with exhaustion, as he pulled his blanket over him he slumped to the ground fast asleep.

The few remaining monsters waited for a few minutes before moving in for the kill.

MILLICENT'S LAIR.

Millicent's lair in the mountains was a huge, very dark and very damp cave. The mouth of the cave opened up onto a large clearing where the Dark and Scary Forest met the mountain range. In the middle of the clearing was a very large black rock. Scattered around the clearing were a good many tree stumps showing signs of being burnt rather than cut. All this gave the clearing a very eerie atmosphere.

A damp cave is not altogether a wise choice of abode for a dragon, because dragons are very susceptible to catching colds. I am sure your mother has told you many times to stay out of damp caves or you will catch a "dragon sized cold." There again Millicent's cave was not all bad, it did have enough room for her to be comfortable and as it burrowed deep into the mountain-side, it twisted and turned offering plenty of hiding spaces and making it quite easy to get lost if you didn't know your way around.

Millicent had not bothered to find a drier cave, for a couple of reasons, the first being there are not many dragon sized caves, outside the dragon colony. The dragon colony lay deeper in the heart of the mountains where humans rarely ventured or returned. The second being she was not overly keen on moving back to or even visiting the dragon colony.

After all the flying about terrorizing the people of Lassaggnee and the castle, collecting a few of the people and some other things to eat, Millicent was tired. She was so tired she had not even bothered to eat any of the people, or other things, she had gathered. After making sure her captives were sufficiently incapable of finding their way out of the cave, Millicent took a nap.

A nap for you or I would last an hour or so but for a dragon a nap can last a few days, usually. Millicent was only able to sleep for about two days.

As you may know dragons have very sensitive hearing and as Millicent was not used to having company, it was hard for her to settle down and sleep because her captives were busy complaining. They complained about the darkness, they complained about the dampness, they complained about being held captive, they complained about being herded out into the clearing and made to pick copious amounts of nuts and berries, they complained about having nothing but nuts and berries to eat, on and on they complained. They only stopped complaining after Millicent threatened to start eating them if they did not stop.

They stopped complaining, they only stopped for a few more days however. Well, most of them stopped, the others just whispered their complaints. Then the sneezing started. The sneezing just gave the captives even more to complain about, especially Princess Maybel.

Princess Maybel was sitting on a rock deep inside Millicent's cave and was fussing with her wedding dress. While she was thankful for not having to get married to Prince Colah, or being eaten, she was upset about her dress being ruined. After all, it was a lovely dress and it did make her feel extra special, so now she was in a foul mood, and made sure everyone knew it.

A huge ball of flame rolled along the roof of the cave.

Maybel could see that her once white dress was now covered in splotches of soot. The splotches of soot did nothing to calm the petulant princess.

"Will somebody tell that dragon to stop sneezing? Every time she does, I get more soot on my dress. It's just not good enough," Maybel said petulantly.

"Will you shut up about your rotten dress." an equally bad tempered voice came from the shadows.

"How dare you talk to me like that? I am the Princess and..."

"My Daddy is the King...," another voice mocked from the shadows.

"And he'll have you thrown into the deepest dungeon..." mocked yet another voice.

"Will you all be...ahh...be...ahh...aaaaCHOOOOOOOO... quiet?"

Millicent sneezed again, sending, yet another, ball of flame rolling across the roof of the cavern.

Princess Maybel turned to glare at the group of people huddled behind her rock. The group of people huddled behind her rock did not see Maybel's glare because the ball of flame had extinguished, and once again, the cave was plunged into darkness. Even if they had seen the princess' glare, they would have ignored it.

"Just you wait. Prince Colah will be here any minute to rescue me, and then you'll be in trouble." Maybel threatened.

"Ha! Fat chance! That little weasel is probably hiding behind one of those tapestries in the castle," a female voice sneered from the darkness.

"If you dohh...dohhhn...AAAAAAAAAAACHOOOOOO!' Another ball of flame rolled along the roof of the cave.

"If you don't pipe down I'll come down there and roast all of you nowwaaaaaaaaachoooooooooooooooooo!" Millicent sneezed.

"Why?" a small voice asked.

"Why whaaa...whaaa...what?" Millicent asked, stifling yet another sneeze.

"Why should we be quiet?" the small voice inquired.

"Because I said so, and I'm trying to get some sleep." Millicent answered.

"Why?" the small voice asked again.

"AAAAAACHOOOOO. Why am I trying to get some sleep?" Millicent asked.

"No." the small voice answered.

"Why what, then?" asked Millicent sounding a little confused.

"Why won't you let us go?" the small voice asked.

"I would have thought the answer to that would be... be... AHOB... AAAAAACHOOOO ...obvious," sneezed Millicent.

"Not to me," said the small voice.

"I know, I know!" another voice eagerly exclaimed.

"Well why don't you tell us then," somebody else said sarcastically.

"It's because, because… because she doesn't want us to tell everyone where she lives, because if everyone knew where she lived, she'd have hordes of tourists trampling through her cave wanting her to pose for pictures with their families, and they'd drop lots of rubbish, and mess up her cave, and…"

"Oh do shut up!" snapped Maybel.

"I don't think that's very nice," the eager voice said, though not so eagerly. "Was I right though?"

"Not really," Millicent replied.

"Was I close?"

"No."

"No?"

"No."

"Oh. So what, then?"

"Let me try to make it very simple for you. I'm a dragon, you're a human, and dragons typically eat humans, among other things," Millicent explained.

"Oh. So you don't care about tourists coming into your cave then?"

"Bring them on! I won't have to get out of bed. I can just cook them as they pose for their pictures."

"That won't be very good for business. You won't get many repeat customers," a knowing voice commented.

"Really. What a shame," Millicent said snidely.

Millicent did not want to eat the humans; she had in fact become quite lonely having left the dragon colony, many, many years before.

Millicent had not left the dragon colony under happy circumstances; she had left because all of the other dragons had teased her for being different. She was not different because of the way she looked, she was not different because of the way she spoke, she was not different because of the way she walked, or anything like that. Millicent was different from the other dragons because she did not like to eat meat.

Millicent was a vegetarian.

When Millicent was just a hatchling, she woke up early one morning and looked over to where her mother was preparing breakfast. Mother dragons do not prepare breakfast like your mother prepares your breakfast. Mother dragons go out very early and catch whatever creature they can and then... I will spare you the details, but I will say that it is not something a very young hatchling, or human child, should ever see. Millicent was so shocked by what she saw that morning that she refused to eat with the other dragon babies ever again. Every morning she would take her food outside, bury it, and then look for berries or other plant-based foods. One day, one of the other young dragons, Phoebe, followed Millicent out of the cave and hid out of sight. When she saw Millicent let her meal go -they were old enough for live prey at the time- and then collect all sorts of nuts and berries to eat, Phoebe flew back to the cave to tell the others.

At first, it was only the young dragons that teased Millicent; they only did so when there were no adults about. But one day, one of Millicent's uncles came home from work early and over-heard the taunting. Uncle Theodore took Millicent aside and asked her if it was true, when she admitted she was a "vegigon" –as the other kids called her- he smiled kindly and told her not to let anyone else know. Strangely, she felt much better, now that an adult knew her secret and an adult that seemed to be sympathetic. But a few weeks later during a hatchday party for Phoebe, Uncle Theodore –not realizing Millicent was standing behind him- made a mean joke about vegigons, and all of the younger dragons pointed at Millicent and laughed, worse so did a lot of the grownups. Millicent's scales turned bright yellow – a sure sign a dragon is very embarrassed- she turned and flew out of the cave and away from the colony forever. Some of the younger dragons took off after her; not to ask her to come back, they just wanted to tease her even more.

When Millicent did not return after a few hours, her parents, and Uncle Theodore, became very worried. They spent weeks searching for her. Unfortunately, they were trapped by dragon hunters and were sold to a zoo in a far, far away place. Uncle Theodore ended up having to take part in a strange competition at some equally strange, magical school.

As far as Millicent knew, she was the only vegigon in the world, and her family did not care about her anymore, which made her feel even lonelier.

She was not, and they did, but that is another story for another day.

"Hey, wait a minute. You've stopped sneezing." said one of the voices from the dark.

"So I have. Well you know what that means don't you?" Millicent asked no one in particular.

"Er... No," several voices replied.

"Well you would if you had studied your dragon mythology better." Millicent scolded.

"So what does it mean then?" the small voice asked.

"It means that some fool has come to rescue you."

"See...I knew that my daddy would send Prince Colah to rescue me." Maybel sneered.

"Oh shut up!" everybody yelled, including Millicent.

"Anyway it's not a prince." Millicent informed them.

"How do you know?" the knowing voice asked in a disbelieving tone.

"Because she hasn't come out in a rash." a brand new voice, which sounded like it came from the mouth of the cave, said.

"Now that's someone who has studied his dragon mythology," said Millicent, as she flew out of the cave.

KEVIN MAKES A NEW FRIEND .

King Archibald's patience was wearing very thin, he was getting more and more frustrated and worried about the lack of news from the spies he had sent after Prince Gaston and Kevin. He did get the news about Prince Gaston taking off for his own home and leaving Kevin to deal with the dragon all by himself. He also heard that the spy assigned to Prince Gaston had decided that life was better in the kingdom of Arabacca and was not going to return.

King Archibald received a fairly accurate account of Kevin's visit to the Big Bore, though that particular spy did seem to be suffering from a very bad headache. The spy had also managed to lose track of Kevin when Kevin left the bar. The spy claimed it was due to the patrons insisting he stay for "just one more drink." It is safe to say that that particular spy's career came to a crashing halt in the dungeons a few seconds after he finished his report.

The spy assigned to watch the other spies was more experienced and decided not to bother chasing Prince Gaston but to stick with Kevin and not go into the Big Bore. A very wise decision.

When Kevin left the Big Bore and walked off into the night, the spy, whose name was Smiler LeCarry, followed as best he could. The next morning, as Kevin was picking thorns out of his hair, Smiler was struggling to free his clothing from the thorns of the "Longthorn Rose" bush he had slept under.

When Smiler saw Kevin curl up under a patch of rose bushes across the lane, he thought that Kevin had made a bad choice, as he (Smiler) had found a nice grassy patch under the shelter of a thorn less bush. The next morning Smiler realized his mistake and learned a valuable lesson in knowing your surroundings.

The Longthorn Rose is very well named as its thorns can grow to several inches especially when it feels threatened. During the night, the Longthorn's thorns had grown and were just starting to break Smiler's skin when he woke up. He was lucky. While he was freeing himself from the thorns, he looked over to where Kevin had been lying.

Kevin was gone.

Once free of the thorns and having managed to get most of his clothing back, although it was rather tattered, Smiler ran down the lane hoping to find Kevin.

Before he ran down the lane, he sent a message back to the castle using a homing frog. Homing frogs are specially trained frogs that no matter where they are they can always find their way back home. Unlike homing pigeons, homing frogs can travel in any kind of weather, except for extreme cold. In extreme cold, the frogs were substituted with homing ferrets. You might be thinking homing ferrets would be perfect any time of year, not quite, in warmer weather they become very unreliable, as they tend to wander off down the nearest rabbit hole. When the homing frog reached the castle and had delivered its message, it was rewarded with a feast of flies. One more note, about homing frogs, they were regarded as traitors by the wild frogs. The homing frogs were often much bigger, because all their food was provided, so the wild frogs tended to ignore the "homers" rather than confront them. Even if a homer were in trouble, the wild frogs would not help.

The latest homing frog message however did not alleviate King Archibald's fears. If anything, the message only served to make him even more anxious. His grand plan was not working as well as he would have liked. Instead of Prince Gaston returning with Princess Maybel, it looked like no one was going to. King Archibald had little or no faith in Kevin's ability to rescue the princess. On the other hand, if Kevin did rescue Princess Maybel, that would probably mean they would want to get married. The idea of his daughter marrying a commoner was almost more unbearable than the thought of never seeing her again, or worse yet someone calling him Archie. King Archibald decided to start making some changes to his plans.

A day or so later, another homing frog came hopping into the castle. The new message was even less encouraging. Kevin had entered the Dark and Scary Forest, no one in living memory had ever come out again. King Archibald decided to send the best members of the king's guard to Spag-Bol, the closest village to the Dark and Scary Forest. From there they were to make plans to organize a search for the dragon's lair and rescue the princess.

Smiler LeCarry followed Kevin into the Dark and Scary Forest. Trying to follow Kevin and stay out of sight while twisting around the trees was not exactly easy. At one point, both Kevin and Smiler were walking around and around the base of the same massive tree. Kevin did not know Smiler was there and Smiler was trying to keep it that way, his tattered clothing helped as it disguised Smiler's shape.

The tattered clothing also helped Smiler from being noticed by the monsters. The monsters were so unused to any humans entering the forest that they fixated only on Kevin. Smiler though still kept one watchful eye on the monsters.

When Kevin retrieved his compass from his satchel, Smiler's opinion of Kevin shifted. As they wound their way through the Dark and Scary Forest Smiler realized that Kevin seemed to know what he was doing and where he was going. When they got to the clearing, Smiler stayed hidden as Kevin gathered firewood, he was puzzled when Kevin became obviously excited and started picking all of the tiny roses that grew around the edge of the clearing. Smiler searched his memory and then it hit him, he knew exactly why Kevin had got so excited about the roses, he did not quite believe it, but he did understand. Once again, Smiler's opinion of Kevin shifted. He began to think that maybe, just maybe Kevin stood a chance of saving the princess, if he survived the Dark and Scary Forest.

Smiler watched Kevin build a very big fire in the center of the clearing. When Kevin unwrapped, his bread and cheese Smiler realized that he had no eaten for sometime either. Smiler tried to ignore his grumbling stomach as he noticed the monsters creep closer to the edge of the forest. When he saw Kevin nodding off and suddenly jumping up trying so very hard to stay awake, Smiler was tempted to run into the clearing to help Kevin, and maybe grab a bite of bread and cheese. Despite his hunger Smiler knew that his orders were not to get involved, he was to just observe and report. So he observed from afar, as the monsters stepped closer each time Kevin nodded off and retreat when Kevin jumped up. But soon Smiler was fighting his own fatigue, he climbed a tree to keep away from the monsters, he knew they would soon find his scent. Smiler found a nice broad branch to get comfortable on that also kept Kevin in view. The last thing Smiler remembered was seeing Kevin once again stand up and walk around the fire that was now beginning to die out. Smiler fell asleep.

The next morning Smiler woke with a start and almost fell out of his tree. He quickly looked over to where Kevin had been and all he saw was a blackened circle with a few wisps of smoke curling up into the cool morning air. Kevin was gone.

Smiler scrambled down from his tree and ran into the clearing, he carefully walked around the remains of the fire trying to see if there were any clues to what had happened to Kevin. All he could find were hundreds of odd footprints, some of the footprints were quite monstrous. Also, there were splotches of what looked like blood and bits of bone, scattered all around the remains of the fire, like something or somebody had been torn apart.

Fearing the worst Smiler walked around the still smoldering fire one more time, hoping to find a clue that Kevin had survived the night. Not really looking where he was going Smiler tripped over something. Something that grunted. Smiler looked around expecting to see a boulder or something that could have tripped him. He only saw the trampled grass around the fire. Then suddenly a hole appeared in the grass and Kevin rolled out of the hole. Rubbing his eyes and stretching, Kevin stood up and proceeded to fold up the blanket that had suddenly taken the place of the hole. Kevin sensed he was being watched. He turned slowly around and looked at Smiler. Smiler was staring dumbfounded at Kevin. Kevin looked at Smiler and then a smile of realization crossed Kevin's face.

"Hello." Kevin said.

"Hello." Smiler replied staring at the blanket.

"It's a Hide-a-way…" Kevin started to explain.

"I know. I've heard of them, seen the ads, but always thought those ads were fake, you know the ads they put in the back of those 'Fantastical Tales' books…" Smiler's disbelief in what he saw amused Kevin.

"That's how I got mine a few years ago, unbelievable and a great bargain I think, now. It took me some time to save the six pentsos and three qgdgts. The three qgdgts was the hardest part…"

"So the monsters…?"

"Trampled all over me but never found me, they were getting in each other's way and sniffing but…"

"They must've been so frustrated…"

"Yep. They started fighting among themselves and it looks to me like they…"

"…ate each other?

"You could be right, except there must be at least one left over, lurking in the dark."

"Well I think it's safe to say that one will be sleeping off one big meal for a few days."

Kevin and Smiler, chuckled at the thought.

"You know Kevin, you are full of surprises. Do you think you ate enough of the dragon roses?"

"I'm not sure, I'll have some more for breakfast, wanna try some? By the way how was your night under the Longthons?" Kevin asked, looking at Smiler's shredded clothes.

"Lovely, thanks, the wake up was a little rough. And I'll say no thanks to the dragon roses but I wouldn't pass up some bread and cheese, if you can spare some?" Smiler said hungrily.

Kevin reached into his satchel and once again pulled out the napkin with the bread and cheese wrapped in it. To Smiler's great surprise the loaf of bread and round of cheese appeared to have never been touched.

"It seems to me you're well prepared, better than I am at least. How do you intend to deal with the dragon, what's your plan?"

"Well that depends on you, are you willing to help?"

"Certainly, if it means getting the princess back so she can marry Prince…"

"Ah. About that. That doesn't fit my plan exactly."

"Oh?"

"Look I need to know if I can trust you?"

"I'm a spy."

"I see what you mean. Well I can either enlist your help or…"

"As my orders were to only observe, report back to Archie and, if necessary, make sure Princess Maybel is safely returned to the castle…"

"So if I rescue Princess Maybel…?"

"It'll make my job easier, and, like I said you seem equipped to do the job, plus your motivation is much purer than mine."

"Alright, if you promise to not get in the way."

"By the way do you have anything to drink, my water pouch got ripped by the Longthorns?"

"Certainly!" Exclaimed Kevin as he pulled what looked like an empty water pouch from his satchel.

"But it's empty…"

"Really? Take the cork out and try."

Smiler did as instructed and lifted the pouch to his lips, a stream of the purest, cleanest water he had ever drank flowed from the spout. It stopped the moment he removed it from his lips.

"Unbelievable. Another Fantastical Tales purchase?"

Kevin just smiled.

"So do you promise…?"

"I so promise, heck I might even help, I like you Kevin."

"Thanks, the feeling is mutual. So here's my plan…"

Kevin and Smiler sat down and broke bread, and cheese and drank cool clear water. Smiler even tried one of the Dragon Roses but spat it out. Kevin smiled, as he ate more, he was beginning to acquire a taste for them. Kevin, having survived the Dark and Scary forest and found the Dragon Roses had also found a new level of self confidence. Over breakfast, Kevin laid out his plan including where Smiler could help. When they were done, they shook hands and left the clearing going in different directions.

A few hours later, an exhausted homing frog hopped in through the front gate of the castle. The frog's message did little to relieve King Archibald's fears, so he sent an urgent message to the soldiers he had sent to Spag-Bol, they were to go into the Dark and Scary Forest and find Princess Maybel or never return.

KEVIN AND MILLICENT MEET.

Kevin, even more confident than ever, worked his way through the rest of the still dark but not so scary forest. He soon came upon another clearing. This one was at least three times bigger than the first one and had a huge blackened rock standing in the middle of it. All over the clearing were the stumps of trees that had been burned away, even the grass seemed to be a little charred. On the other side of the clearing Kevin saw what he hopped he would see. The mouth of a massive cave. Every so often, a small trickle of smoke would twist its way out and head skyward. The trickles of smoke were accompanied by the distinctive, yet muffled, sounds of dragon sneezes.

Kevin gingerly picked his way into the cave. He stopped at the sound of voices. Then the sneezing stopped. Kevin knew that the dragon knew he was there. When he called out, "Because she hasn't come out in a rash." he had already turned and headed for the mouth of the cave.

Kevin was standing just inside the mouth of the cave when he saw Millicent heading straight for him, blowing small balls of fire at him. Kevin managed to bob and weave out of the way of the fireballs as he ran away. Dodging a huge fireball Kevin scrambled up onto the huge rock in the center of the clearing. Millicent blew another fireball at Kevin. Kevin ducked but then made the mistake of standing up again. Just as he stood up and before he could react Millicent spat a massive fireball that engulfed the rock and Kevin.

Millicent's captives had run after Millicent, and when they got to the mouth of the cave, they saw her turn from a mile or so out and head back to the cave, as a huge fireball engulfed the very large, very black rock. When the fireball died out, they saw what looked like the charred figure of a man standing on the rock. Little bits of fire flickered on his clothing as the overcooked figure wavered in the breeze. Their hopes dashed, the small band of people slowly turned back into the cave.

"Hang on. He's moving," said the eager voice, which everyone could now see belonged to a young boy.

They all turned to look, and sure enough, the charred figure was moving and oddly, was laughing. Even more oddly, he seemed to be dancing a little jig.

"Hey dragon! Nice try!" Kevin jeered at the dragon. Little wisps of smoke drifted out of his mouth as he spoke.

Millicent stopped and hovered just in front of the charred figure.

"I see someone's been eating his dragon roses, and the name is Millicent." said Millicent as she glided around the huge rock.

"I'm sorry, good morning Millicent. You know, I didn't totally believe they'd work, until now," Kevin said, slapping out the little bits of fire on his clothes.

"They do, and good morning to you." Millicent said, disappointment in her voice.

"Apparently very well. That is so cool!" exclaimed Kevin.

"And I suppose you've already rubbed Otter Oil onto your sword?" Millicent asked.

"Naturally," Kevin answered.

"So I don't stand much chance of beating you then? Unless..."

"Unless what?" asked Kevin.

"Oh, I was just wondering when you got the otter oil."

"In the spring," Kevin answered.

Millicent let out a victorious howl and dove straight at Kevin. Kevin leapt off his boulder and ran into the cave, passed the startled onlookers, and kept going. Millicent streaked in overhead and barely made the turn into the heart of the cave. A short while later, the little crowd heard a terrible scream and then nothing happened.

After a few more minutes of nothing happening, they quietly

crept away from the cave and started to look for a way through the Dark and Scary Forest. They were glad to be free, but couldn't help being sad for the brave young man who had tried to save them. Maybel was unable to recognize him under all the soot, though she thought his voice sounded familiar but in the confusion could not put two and two together. She did feel sorry for the young man but was happy she was free. That was until the knowing voice, which belonged to Grean-the-Grocer, said, "Poor Kevin. He wasn't a bad lad... just a bit slow on the uptake."

"I never saw him as a hero, though," the bad tempered voice said, which belonged to Blough-the-glassmaker.

"What are you talking about?" the Princess demanded.

"That lad that just saved us. It was Kevin Plane," Blough-the-glassmaker replied.

"Kevin?" the Princess asked quietly.

"Yes, Princess."

"The same Kevin that drooled at me?" Princess Maybel sniffled, tears welling up in her eyes.

"Yes Princess. I'm sorry. Did you know him well?" a gentle voice asked, which belonged to her dressmaker Sue Inng.

"No, I didn't know him, I..." the Princess sobbed.

"Well why are you crying like you've just lost the love of your life?" Sue Inng asked.

"Because he was just that."

"But how...? I mean, if you didn't know...?"

"We just knew the moment our eyes met. And, even though we had only spent a few brief moments in the dungeon before he was locked away in that awful tower, we still knew that we are ...were... meant to be together."

"Oh that's silly! That sort of thing is fine for the storybooks but it never happens in real life," Blough-the-glassmaker grumbled.

"Just because it never happened for you..." Princess Maybel began.

Before Blough-the-glassmaker could think of a snappy retort,

Millicent flew out of the cave and landed with a heavy thud in front of them, smoke drifting from her nostrils victoriously.

"And just where do you think you are going?" she inquired.

"Er… well… um… that is… we thought that as you were busy with Kevin, we'd get out of your way and sort of go home." Grean-the-Grocer tried.

"Oh really? Well I have a little surprise waiting for you. I'm even hungrier now, so get back inside before I roast the lot of you on the spot." As Millicent spoke, she let a trickle of fire escape from her nostrils; none of her captives knew she was a vegigon. They all assumed that the vast quantities of berries and nuts, they were made to gather, were so they could be fattened up for when Millicent was ready to eat them. When she set fire to a tree and then ate it they thought she was just trying to scare them some more.

Millicent noticed that the Princess was crying on Sue Inng's shoulder.

"What are you crying for?" Millicent demanded.

Princess Maybel stopped crying and glared venomously at Millicent.

"You killed the only person I ever loved and when I get back to the castle I'm going to make my father send every soldier in the kingdom to hunt you down like the dirty dragon you are."

"I never touched your precious little Prince Soda or whatever his name is," Millicent said indignantly.

"I'm not talking about that weasel; I couldn't care less about him…" Princess Maybel sobbed.

"You were going to marry him, weren't you?" Asked Millicent

"Yes, but I don't love him. My father was forcing me to marry him."

"Well then why didn't you run away or something?" Millicent challenged.

"I was running away, when you came along and picked me up. Why do you think I was running away from the castle and not toward it, like everyone else?" the Princess snapped, beginning to get angry again.

"Very convenient. And I'm supposed to believe you?" Millicent sneered.

"Yes," said the princess simply.

"Well, it really doesn't matter now, does it? So why don't you and your little friends run along back inside like good dragon fodder?"

"Because we don't want to?" tried Blough-the-glassmaker.

His answer was a very small ball of fire that singed his hair, a little, but enough to make him and the others scurry back into the cave. Grean-the-grocer went first, in the hope of finding Kevin's remains before the Princess saw them. However, grope around in the dark as hard as he could, he found no trace of Kevin. Mind you, it did not help that the cave was still as dark as dark can be.

Millicent stomped into the cave behind, herding them like cattle. Once they were all inside the depths of the cave, Millicent sneezed a sneeze so big that it sent a huger-than-huge fireball up to the roof of the cave. The fireball seemed to hang there for a very long time before it finally went out. It lit up the cave long enough for everybody to have a good look around for Kevin, or rather what they thought might remain of Kevin.

Princess Maybel was just about to yell at the extremely sooty person standing next to her, making her dress even dirtier, when she let out a loud squeal.

"KEVIN!" she squealed and threw her arms around his neck. Then she let go and hit him as hard as she could.

It was at that moment that the fireball went out.

"OUCH! That hurt! Millicent, will you please light up this cave again?" Kevin asked.

Millicent obliged and Maybel hit Kevin again. Kevin fell over and Maybel quickly knelt down beside him.

"Oh Kevin, I'm sorry! Are you all right?" Maybel's voice was full of genuine concern as she helped Kevin to his feet.

"I wish I'd thought of doing that," Millicent muttered.

"Oh come on now, it wouldn't have made any difference. I still would've been able to prick you with my sword," Kevin told her.

"Humph," said Millicent.

"Anyway, why'd you hit me?" Kevin asked of Maybel.

"Because I thought you were dead but you weren't, so I hit you to make sure."

By this time, the rest of Millicent's captives had gathered around Kevin and were showering him with questions. Kevin explained that when Millicent had chased him inside, he had clambered up the side of the cave, and as she flew by, he nicked her with his sword. Kevin went on to explain about some of the books he had read while sitting in the Tall Tower. How they taught him all about the Dragon Roses and the Otter Oil and so on.

But you probably do not want to bother with the details. Do you? Well in case you do, here they are. You can skip this part if you want to but then you will never know, will you?

Dragon Roses grow only in the Kingdom of Blognasee, to be more precise only the Dark and Scary Forest and then only on the edges of clearings that were created by a dragon. So they are very rare but extremely useful when one has to go up against a dragon. Apart from providing an excellent source of nutrition, Dragon Roses will actually protect you from a dragon's fireballs. It's some sort of chemical reaction thing that I do not understand, but it seems to work. As you already know, the Dragon Roses taste terrible and to be effective you have to eat a lot of them. Obviously, Kevin did eat a lot of them.

Otter Oil, as you may already know, has some very powerful properties when it comes to dealing with dragons. If it gets into their blood, it compels them to obey, without question, the person who put the Otter Oil into their system. Before you go dashing off to find some Otter Oil, and try to tame a few dragons, there are a couple of details you need to know. The foremost detail is that whenever you find yourself fighting with a dragon and you intend on using Otter Oil, you have to tell the truth, or the Otter Oil will work in reverse. The second thing you need to know is that the Otter Oil can only be harvested in the autumn, or more precisely on the 22nd of September.

Now if you remember, Millicent said to Kevin, "Oh, I was just wondering when you got the Otter Oil..." and Kevin said to Millicent "In the spring." which is not the right time of year. So now you are probably thinking that Kevin was either not exactly truthful and that the oil should not have worked, or that if he did get the oil in the spring, it should not have worked either. Well, that would be true, but unfortunately, for Millicent, she had not quite asked the right question.

You see Kevin did get the Otter Oil during the spring, but he had bought it from a merchant who was staying at The Big Bore Inn. The merchant had bought the Otter Oil from an old Otter Oil harvester. The Otter Oil harvester was old, not the otter or the oil. The old Otter Oil harvester had harvested the Otter Oil on the third Monday of September of the previous year, which luckily for Kevin happened to be the 22nd of September. Oh by the way, it has to be on a Monday. Otherwise, it works in reverse.

Therefore, Kevin did not lie to Millicent; all he did was answer her question, which led her to believe that the Otter Oil was impotent. That is why, when Kevin said "In the spring," Millicent flew at him, thinking she was going to win the battle. What Millicent should have asked was "Oh I was just wondering when the Otter Oil was harvested...?" but she did not. If she had, this story would have ended a while ago.

By the way, the terrible scream came from Millicent when she was nicked by Kevin's sword. It did not really hurt her, but when she felt the Otter Oil in her blood, she was very, very disappointed. One last thing: harvesting Otter Oil does not harm the otters at all. In fact, the otters kind of like it. If you really want to know how to harvest Otter Oil, I will tell you, but we have to be quick, as they are all waiting for us. To harvest Otter Oil you get a piece of wood (nowadays you can get plastic ones) that has a row of sharp tines about an inch long, and set very close to each other. Using your comb -that is what those things are called- you comb the Otter and let the oil they use to keep their fur waterproof, drip from the comb into a container of your choice. Removing the Otter Oil from the Otter's coat in no way reduces the waterproof qualities of their fur, because they have a special gland that replenishes the oil as needed, in fact it helps them keep their fur clean as the comb will catch any bugs that maybe residing in the otter's fur.

Shall we continue with the story?

Wait a minute… there is nobody in the cave. They must have gone on by themselves. We will catch up with them later. Let us see what Archie's up to.

THE ROYAL WEDDING.

King Archibald had not slept a wink since the last of the homing frogs had delivered its message, three days ago. As a result, he did not look very good -in fact the phrase "extremely disheveled" comes to mind- and his temper was even worse. His temper was so bad the dungeons were now packed with people, because even looking at the king was punishable by a lengthy stay in the deepest dungeon, plus six pokes-in-the-eye-with-a-sharp-stick. However, because poking-in-the-eye-with-a-sharp-stick was banned by law, King Archibald had to be satisfied with sentencing people to thirteen slaps-in-the-face-with-a-wet-fish.

That soon became problematic because there had been so many people given the same sentence, that Morry-the-executioner (who didn't really do any actual "executions" but did carry out the orders to slap people in the face with a wet fish, which is sometimes called "executing an order") had run out of fish. Morry was also the village fishmonger, so was sometimes called Morry-the-fish. Apparently, the law insists upon using only fresh fish for each slap, so it is easy to see why Morry-the-fish ran out of fish. Morry-the-fish did try using eels but found that it was not possible to get a really good grip. Morry-the-fish's experiment with eels did not last long enough to justify yet another name; anyway, I think Morry-the-eel is a rather silly name. Secretly, Morry-the-fish was glad of the lack of fish, as she was getting very tired, even happier were those who had been sentenced to, thirteen slaps-in-the-face-with-a-wet-fish.

The three footmen were happy with the situation because they had the only bath, and were making a small fortune by renting it to those who wanted to wash off the daily grime and the smell of fish. Johnson and the other two guards had been told to return to duty, which to them was worse than being in the dungeon. At least in the dungeon they were safe from any dragons, did not have to do any work, and could have a bath instead of sharing the barrack bucket.

Back in the throne room, King Archibald was pacing back and forth in front of his throne. He was trying to work out whether he was happy, or not, that Prince Gaston had gone home and now Kevin had disappeared. For all King Archibald knew Kevin was either lost in the Dark and Scary Forest or was currently residing in the dragon's stomach.

King Archibald was not ready to admit defeat yet, despite news that the spy, Smiler LeCarry, had emerged from the forest dressed only in a few rags, babbling about the monsters of the Dark and Scary Forest and had then turned around only to run back into the darkness. This had unnerved the soldiers who had just arrived from Spag-Bol, so much that they refused to go into the forest.

Somehow, King Archibald knew Princess Maybel was going to be all right, and would return. Still he was beginning to wonder, especially as nobody had spoken to him for the last couple of days.

Nobody had spoken to him for the last couple of days because nobody wanted to be sent to the overcrowded dungeon. Saying anything to the King was an instant 'get thrown in the dungeon and twenty-six slaps-in-the-face-with-a-wet-fish' offense, so the people in the castle now just slipped notes under his door and ran.

One such note was slipped under his door.

King Archibald picked up the note and opened it. Half a second later, even before the note hit the floor, he was running down the corridor and into the main hall. The main hall was where everyone else, apart from the ones in the dungeon, had decided to hide from the king. When he burst through the door, the room at first appeared to be empty. The king looked around the room and found exactly what he was looking for: a pair of shoes. A pair of shoes that was very hard to miss, as they were a particularly virulent shade of purple.

The King stopped in front of the tapestry the shoes were sticking out from. The shoes belonged to the Chancellor and were very easy to spot, not just because of the color. They were also the largest pair of shoes, among hundreds of others, which appeared to be neatly arranged below each of the tapestries lining the walls of the main hall. The shoes though were not alone: each pair was accompanied by its owner.

When they heard the King running down the corridor, every person in the room had the same idea, and ran for cover behind the tapestries.

"Frank, get out here now, and start the wedding proceedings again. Princess Maybel has escaped the dragon! Where's the Captain-of-the-Guard?" The King was, to say the least, a little excited.

"He's in the dungeon," a muffled voice said from behind one of the tapestries.

"Well don't just hide there! Go and get him, and tell him to send his best men to collect my daughter from Spag-Bol..."

"Err...don't you mean his second best? You already sent the bes...," said a voice from behind a tapestry across the room.

"You did not just interrupt me did you?" snarled the king.

"The princess is waiting at the Balls Head Inn." another one of Diz Slexia's signs. The king continued, as there was no reply.

"Send the gold carriage to bring her home and make sure it is heavily guarded," ordered the king.

"Why are you still here? Frank... Frankie, come on out. You don't have to hide anymore," encouraged the king.

The Chancellor slithered out from behind the tapestry and instantly the king regretted not shading his eyes in time. Frank was still wearing his new outfit that he had commissioned for the wedding. Even though he had been wearing it for a few days, and it had become a little grimy, it was still a spectacularly brilliant color. The color clashed wonderfully with his shoes and came close to being exactly the wrong color for him to be wearing, considering the new color of his hair. Let us just say that there are certain shades of green, orange and purple that should never be in the same room with each other.

The King noticed another pair of feet that looked suspiciously like the Captain-of-the-Guard's. The shiny boots ran towards the door, without coming out from behind the tapestries, suddenly there were a lot of shoes hoping up and down beneath the tapestries and the sound of people upset at having their toes trampled.

"By the way, Captain, find that fool Prince Copa or whatever his name is, and get him ready for the wedding ceremony," the King called after the rapidly retreating pair of boots.

It took the Captain and almost all of the other soldiers several hours to find and extract Prince Colah from his hideout under a pile of hay bales in the stables.

In case you are wondering, Prince Colah's entourage had already returned to their homeland, having completed their given task of escorting the prince around the known world until he found a bride. Nobody had said they had to stick around for the wedding.

On the morning of Princess Maybel's return from Spag-Bol, everyone had changed into nice clean clothes, and gathered in the courtyard to greet the Princess upon her arrival.

King Archibald not leaving anything to chance, wanted to get Princess Maybel and Prince Colah married without any delay. Therefore, he had arranged for the wedding ceremony to start as soon as Princess Maybel arrived.

When the carriages carrying Princess Maybel and the rest of her fellow ex-dragon-captives rolled through the village and into the courtyard, a huge cheer went up from the crowd.

A red carpet had been carefully laid in a straight line from the huge ornate doorway, down the wide staircase and halfway across the courtyard. As King Archie quickly walked down the carpet to greet his daughter, he bumped into a tall red thing. The tall red thing was the Chancellor, whose new outfit exactly matched the color and texture of the red carpet. King Archibald majestically shoved the Chancellor out of his way. The Chancellor stumbled forward and promptly had his toes run over by the Princess' carriage, as its drivers were trying to line up the door of the carriage with the carpet. Finally, the carriage stopped and the King opened the door. Princess Maybel took his hand and gracefully stepped down from the carriage. Her dress had been cleaned and repaired during her wait in Spag-Bol and she looked, I must admit, every bit the beautiful princess bride that she was. The crowd gasped at the stunning sight and then spontaneously burst into song, singing the Blognasee national anthem.

Prince Colah was awestruck and thought he was definitely the luckiest Prince in the world. As they walked up the carpet towards the royal quarters, the King asked, as nonchalantly as he could, about the fates of the dragon and Kevin. The Princess explained she did not want to talk about it right then and sniffed a little at the mention of Kevin's name.

"Of course not, my dear, we'll talk later," King Archie said consolingly, but he could not resist a small smile of satisfaction.

Now, you might be wondering why Princess Maybel did not mention that Kevin had rescued her and the other villagers. Well, after Kevin had made sure they had met up with, a still very tattered, Smiler at the edge of the Dark and Scary Forest, Kevin explained the rest of his plan and once everyone knew what to do, he told them he was going back to Millicent's cave to look for something. Unfortunately, for Kevin, the Otter Oil had worn off and Millicent was waiting for him. When Kevin entered the cave she pounced, and the last thing the villagers heard from the direction of the mountains was a terrified scream. When they turned to see what had happened, a huge ball of fire lifted up into the clear blue sky.

"That'll be the end of young Kevin's plans then." Blough-the-glassmaker said.

"And Kevin." Added Grean-the-grocer.

Princess Maybel burst into tears and had to be carried away

from the forest.

Princess Maybel was inconsolable for a few days. Smiler had returned to the forest to look for Kevin and slay the dragon but he did not return either. Finally, she was convinced that returning to Lassaggnee and her family was the best thing to do. So a messenger (homing frogs were only used by the spies) was sent to the castle. When the messenger returned to Spag-Bol, he gave the Princess the news that her father was sending his best carriages.

"Oh and your wedding will to happen as soon as you arrive." The messenger added as though it was an afterthought.

By the time they arrived in Lassaggnee, Princess Maybel was resigned to the fact that Kevin was probably dead, and although she would never love another, especially Prince Colah, she might as well be married and live the life her father had planned for her.

So that is how it came to be that King Archibald proudly escorted his daughter through the castle and out the back door. The back door led into the field where the huge tent, freshly covered in roses, had been erected. Meanwhile, everyone else had to run around the outside of the castle to get into the marquee before King Archibald and Princess Maybel. The King and Princess Maybel entered the tent and majestically strolled up the aisle to where Prince Colah, having rushed ahead, was standing grinning from ear to ear at his bride-to-be. His bride-to-be was not smiling, or even blushing, as brides are traditionally expected to do.

As the gentry are so accustomed to doing, both King Archibald and Princess Maybel ignored the fact that everyone else in the tent was panting and wiping the sweat from their brow. When King Archibald and Princess Maybel reached the end of the aisle, King Archibald passed his daughter's hand to Prince Colah. Princess Maybel started to feel a little sick, holding the prince's hand felt like she was holding a cold limp rag. Maybel and Colah turned to face each other and, out of the corner of her eye, Princess Maybel saw a sight that made her smile for the first time in days.

The tent was packed with all of the dignitaries from the King-dom of Blognasee and a few who had come from some of the surrounding kingdoms. Prince Colah's parents had been unable to attend, as they had a prior engagement at their local bingo hall and Prince Andrew was busy arranging the construction of a new bottling plant, but they had sent a representative to make sure... witness the wedding.

Pinoch, the footman with the rather large facial feature, at first felt a bit overdressed and out of place but soon realized that most of the other "royal guests" were also overdressed foot-men or scullery maids. The overdressed footmen and scullery maids were all quite happy to be treated like royalty when they arrived in Lassaggnee, so much so that most of them decided to stay. The real royal guests had, like Prince Colah's parents, per-fectly legitimate reasons for not attending the wedding. Prin-cess Leila of Lyze though had not been able to come up with a truthful excuse so she was the only real royal guest. She also was glad of the opportunity to see Prince Colah married and know that he would not be bothering her again.

Around the edges of the marquee stood the more important people from the village and Maybel noticed her fellow ex-cap-tives were there too. She could also hear the other villagers milling about outside the huge tent, and then suddenly every-one was quiet.

The Bishop of Blognasee, a rather short but very rotund man, stood in front of the bride and groom and started droning on and on about what a beautiful day it was, how beautiful the tent was, and how the congregation looked beautiful, too. He had just finished going on about the beautiful couple standing beau-tifully before him, when he noticed King Archibald was mak-ing a get-on-with-it gesture. For a fleeting moment, the Bishop wondered where Queen Hortense was. The king, however, did not wonder where his queen was. He knew she had insisted on making sure the thirty-four cooks were preparing the wedding feast to her satisfaction. Queen Hortense also felt compelled to taste test everything, several times.

The Bishop started conducting the actual marriage ceremony, which dragged on for another forty-three minutes. The congregation started to get bored and fidgety. Some of the oldest and youngest members of the congregation had fallen asleep. One or two were snoring very loudly. Finally, the Bishop got to the part where he had to ask if the bride and groom knew of any lawful impediment to their marriage. They both said they did not.

The Bishop then asked the congregation the same question. There was silence; even the snoring had stopped. Then suddenly a baby cried and everyone chuckled in relief. The chuckling stopped, however, when a voice from the back of the tent quietly and simply said, "Yes."

THE WEDDING MUST GO ON.

The Bishop stood on tiptoe to see over the heads of the bride and groom, trying to find out where the voice had come from.

"Er... ahem... excuse me, but did someone say 'yes'?" asked the Bishop.

"No, of course not," the King declared jumping to his feet.

"Well, actually, yes, I did," the voice said.

The whole congregation turned to see who had spoken. The person the congregation saw shocked them, but not as much as he shocked the king. King Archibald was so shocked that he could not think what to say. Then he did think what to say, and said it. Actually, he yelled it as loud and as authoritatively as he could.

"GUARDS! GUARDS, SEIZE THAT MAN AND THROW HIM IN THE DUNGEONS NOW!"

Guards from every direction rushed to the back of the tent and were about to "seize that man" -who just happened to be Kevin- when Kevin ran out of the tent, the dark and rather drab cloak he was wearing flapping about him.

The guards chased after him out into the middle of the field, where Kevin suddenly stopped and whistled. Instantly a huge ball of fire engulfed Kevin.

The guards remembered the union specifically forbade them from rushing into a huge ball of fire.

They stopped.

Just before the fireball extinguished, Kevin, dressed in a spectacularly princely suit, walked out of it. Kevin brushed the few charred remains of the rather drab cloak from his shoulders, and nodded politely to the guards. The guards all stared after Kevin with their mouths open and a look of extreme shock and awe on their faces. They had not heard of Dragon Roses and their magical properties. Kevin sauntered back into the tent past the guards, as though it were perfectly normal to walk through great balls of dragon fire.

Kevin strode confidently up to the king, whose face had gone from the bright red of rage to the dark purple of apoplexy.

"Sire…" said Kevin, bowing but not taking his eyes off the king. " I have come to ask for what is rightly mine."

"And just what might that be?" asked King Archibald, thinking quickly and rapidly gaining control of his temper.

"The reward for rescuing the Princess Maybel from the dreaded dragon, Millicent." Kevin said grandiosely.

"Oh! The reward? Yes, yes of course." The relief in the King's voice helped everybody relax, a little. The Chancellor sidled up to the King and whispered in his ear. The King looked at the Chancellor for a second.

"What? No, I'm not going to try and bargain with him; just pay him the requisite amount."

"Excuse me, Sire…" Kevin started.

"You'll get your money and maybe a little extra, but listen, can this wait? We are trying to have a wedding here, or hadn't you noticed?" the King said, beginning to get a tad impatient and gesturing at the tent, guests and all.

"Well, it will be nice to have a dowry, but I don't think you're getting the point," Kevin said calmly.

"Dowry? What are you talking about?" the King asked, becoming more impatient.

"Rule number 47,630,958 part H, of the Rules and Regulations of the…"

"Union?" interrupted the Lieutenant.

The whole congregation turned to stare at the Lieutenant and said,

"What?"

The Lieutenant turned bright red and began looking for the hole he and the Captain-of-the-guard had been looking for earlier in this tale. It did not appear.

Kevin ignored the Lieutenant.

"...Kingdom of Blognasee dated earlier this year, clearly states that 'whomsoever rescues the Princess from a distressful, dastardly or dangerous situation or from any monster, including but not limited to Cyclops, Dragons, Giants, Ogres, Satyrs, Trolls, and or other such mythical or non-mythical beasts, but excluding rabbits, and said beasts must be real and not imagined, is entitled to ask for the aforementioned Princess' hand in marriage" Kevin quoted.

King Archibald turned to a man in a dark suit that had appeared out of nowhere. Eleven more men in dark suits, just as suddenly, joined the first man in the dark suit. The twelve men and their king huddled in a circle while everybody else knowingly whispered, "Lawyers," to each other.

The king, having concluded his conference with the attorneys, turned to face Kevin once again; but, instead of glaring at Kevin, he smiled victoriously.

"What proof do you have that you were in fact the actual rescuer of the princess? As you know rule 47,630,958 part K, clearly states that any rescuer must provide, at least twenty written, eyewitness reports detailing the circumstances of the rescue."

"Oh, right. I almost forgot, here." Kevin pulled twenty-two envelopes from a pocket and handed them to the nearest lawyer.

The lawyer distributed the envelopes among his companions. There was the sound of many envelopes being ripped open and then silence as the letters were read. The lawyer who had been given the letters addressed the king.

"Sire, it appears that all is in order and according to rule 47,630,958 part K-b they have been verified by the..."

"That may be so..." interrupted King Archibald "...but the Princess, according to Rule number 47,630,958 part M, of the Rules and Regulations of the Kingdom of Blognasee, has the option to 'decline any and all proposals of marriage from her rescuer or rescuers -including but not limited to those mortally wounded and or seriously maimed by any monster, including but not limited to Cyclops, Dragons, Giants, Ogres, Satyrs, Trolls, or other such mythical or non-mythical beasts, except rabbits, even if such wounding or maiming occurred during any and all rescue attempts, successful or otherwise.' And as you can see, she is already in the process of marrying Prince Tola here," the King said in a tone that was definite in its finality.

"Er, that's Colah," corrected Prince Colah nervously.

"Whatever," snapped the king.

"Your attorneys are correct. The Princess does have that option..." started Kevin.

"So why doesn't somebody ask her?" an impatient voice from the crowd cried.

Princess Maybel stepped down from the altar to stand beside her father, and smiled lovingly at Kevin. She was so happy to see Kevin alive that she forgot that he was supposed to be dead.

King Archibald looked almost defeated, but there was a tinge of hope in his eyes. Kevin gazed lovingly into Princess Maybel's eyes and drooled a little. They grinned at each other for what felt like a full ten minutes. The crowd was holding its breath, so the only sound was the breeze rustling through the roses adorning the tent. Even the birds had stopped twittering.

Finally, someone gulped in a huge chunk of air and said. "For crying out loud, ask her already yet."

Kevin wiped the drool from his chin, and knelt down on one knee without taking his eyes off the Princess' eyes. The Princess' eyes were brimming with tears of joy as she gave a little nervous laugh its freedom.

"Your most royal and gracious Highness, Princess Maybel of Blognasee..." Kevin said quietly, "...will you do me the greatest of honors by accepting my proposal of marriage?"

A single tear rolled down her face, and Princess Maybel smiled the sunniest smile you could ever imagine, and nodded her head.

"Speak up! Did she say yes?" an old voice asked.

"Yes...! YES! A thousand times yes!" Princess Maybel declared loud and clear.

The crowd erupted with cheers, and laughter, and clapping and dancing, and all sorts of happy carrying on.

Then an extremely loud voice yelled:

"QUIET! "

The crowd quieted down.

"Pray silence for the King!" the loud voice exclaimed, though not so loudly.

King Archibald smiled evilly.

"Well that was beautiful, very touching. There is one thing, though. I hate to bring it up now, but protocol dictates I must. Kevin my boy, did you say the edition of the Rules & Regulations of the Kingdom of Blognasee was the spring edition?" the King said his voice dripping sweetness.

"No, I didn't mention that," Kevin said a little nervously.

The King's smile broadened.

"Ah. I see. But it was that edition you were referring to, no?" asked the King. There was a hint of final victory in his voice.

"That is correct, Sire. The spring edition. Is there a problem?" Kevin asked a slightly more nervous edge to his voice.

"What's wrong?" the Princess was getting very nervous.

The crowd once again held its collective breath.

"Not a big problem as I see it," said the King. "It's just the summer edition of the R.R.K.B. has a revision to rule number...number..." The King turned to the lawyer nearest him. The lawyer started fumbling through a book that was twelve inches thick, by thirteen inches long, by eleven inches wide. The pages of the book were very thin and covered in extraordinarily fine print.

"Er... hah... um... it's number, I've got it right er... um... hah... um... ah... here it is, number 47,630,958 part H. The revision is 47,630,958 part Z-h, Sire."

The crowd breathed out and then in again, and held it again.

"Um... is that the only revision to the spring edition?" Kevin asked more nervously.

Everybody's eyes shifted to the lawyers. The lawyer who had done all the fumbling swallowed nervously.

"Er... yes," he said, confirming it with the other lawyers who either nodded or shrugged an affirmation to him.

"You're quite sure?" asked Kevin.

The lawyers all nodded as noncommittally as possible.

King Archibald thought he detected a rising confidence in Kevin's voice but was certain he was in total control of the situation.

"Good," said the king. "As I was saying, Rule number 47,630,958 part Z-h, states the King may use his discretionary powers and refuse to accept the rescuer's proposal and or deny the rescuer's eligibility if the King feels it appropriate to do so. I hereby do so. Guards arrest Kevin and take him to the dungeon. Maybel, Culpa, back to the altar, please," the King ordered.

"Er... that's Colah," Prince Colah said nervously.

"Like I care..." snarled King Archibald. " Get back up to the altar before I rip your head off!"

The crowd slowly and sadly let out its breath and shuffled back to their seats. Princess Maybel stood still, and then burst into floods of tears. She easily struggled free of Prince Colah's grip as he tried to escort her back to the altar, but the king had hold of her other arm. He half dragged, half carried his inconsolable daughter to the altar.

Twenty-nine heavily armed guards escorted Kevin out of the tent.

THE WEDDING ROUND TWO.

Once again, the Bishop started the ceremony from the top, much to the annoyance of the King, who was still gripping Maybel's arm. For a second time the Bishop reached the question about lawful impediments. Again, the crowd held its breath and tried very hard not to turn and look to the back of the tent. The crowd resumed breathing a few moments later as nothing exciting seemed to be happening.

"I thought we just settled that one?" Prince Colah asked in a puzzled voice.

"We did. Get on with it Bishop!" snapped the King.

"Er... Excuse me..." a now familiar voice called from the back of the tent.

"Kevin!" squealed the Princess happily.

"Kevin?" King Archibald roared angrily.

"Kevin?" exclaimed the shocked congregation.

"Who? What?" a very confused and upset Prince Colah whined.

"GUARDS! GUARDS! GUARDS!" yelled the King.

"They're a little busy right now," said Kevin.

This was true.

The guards were huddled together outside the tent as a trio of fireballs slowly rolled around them. As each fireball died, it was replaced by a fresh one, courtesy of Millicent.

"Listen, you little pipsqueak! We've already settled this..." King Archibald started.

"Actually no, we haven't," interrupted Kevin.

"Don't dare interrupt me again! Yes we did," fumed the King.

"Er No we didn't," replied Kevin, ignoring the threatening nature of the King's voice.

"Yes we did," King Archibald said in a singsong way.

"Didn't," countered Kevin.

"Did," the King

"Didn't," Kevin

"Did."

"Didn't."

This went on for a while until Prince Colah screamed:

"Shut UP!"

The congregation, whose heads had been going back and forth as though they were watching an exceptionally long tennis rally, all settled their gaze upon Prince Colah. Prince Colah went bright red with embarrassment and tried to hide behind the Bishop. It was a rather pointless yet very amusing effort. Imagine a tall thin person standing behind a short and very rotund person. It did serve to relieve the tension in the tent, as everyone had a little chuckle at the sight, even King Archibald smiled.

King Archibald stopped smiling, stormed down the aisle, and stood toe to toe with Kevin. Kevin could feel the king's hot breath on his face, worse yet he could smell it. Kevin considered offering King Archibald a mint, but thought better of it.

"Well you've already disrupted this wedding twice, so we might as well get this over with. There is no way you are going to marry my daughter," King Archibald said very menacingly.

"We'll see. You'd better get your lawyers back in here." Before Kevin had finished speaking, the twelve dark suits had returned and stood behind King Archibald.

"If we're all ready then?" Kevin asked, looking past the king at the lawyers. The lawyers each opened their copies of the R.R.K.B.

"If you'll turn to page 2,340,876, paragraph 45, line 79," Kevin instructed.

The only sounds in the whole kingdom were the gentle breathing of the congregation (the congregation had given up on trying to hold its breath) and the rustling sound of thin paper pages being flipped. Oh, and the occasional soft "whoomp" sound of a new fireball, and some birds twittering in the background and a few other noises that are really quite natural. King Archibald was wondering what the "whoomp" sound was and if it had anything to do with the total absence of his guards.

One by one, the attorneys found the correct page, paragraph, and line. One by one, their faces turned paler and paler as they read. One by one, they slowly backed away from the king and melted into the crowd. The king was still standing nose to nose with Kevin, his face the perfect image of suppressed anger, with a touch of anticipation around the edges.

Slowly, very slowly, the king noticed Kevin's smile had not diminished. In fact, it had broadened. King Archibald's eyes slowly shifted from side to side as he realized he could no longer see the dark suits that had once surrounded him. His expression dissolved very slowly into one of uncertainty and curiosity.

"Will you please read Rule number 387,087,543 part WP574?" Kevin asked the one remaining attorney. The only reason that, that particular attorney had not managed to melt into the crowd was because the King was standing on one of his long-toed shoes.

Every single eye turned to the attorney. The attorney avoided every single eye, especially both of the King's.

"Each edition of the Rules and Regulations of the Kin..." The attorney started in his best courtroom voice.

"Skip that and get to the good bit," Kevin said encouragingly.

"Er... um..." stammered the attorney.

"Just tell us what it says," helped Kevin.

"Well, basically it states that the edition in force at the time any event begins takes precedence over any subsequent edition."

"Which means?" encouraged Kevin.

"It means as the dragon attacked and captured the princess before the new edition was published, any revisions cannot be enforced," stated the lawyer trying to avoid the glaring eyes of his king.

"Thank you. One more thing: when, exactly, was the summer

edition published?" Kevin asked, staring intently at the king. Kevin could see King Archibald's mind was working feverishly to get around this development.

"Er... well, I believe it was actually published this morning," the attorney said, as he retreated out of reach of the King, leaving his shoe behind under the king's foot.

"Thank you. One last thing before you go. Which rule states that if the monarch tries to interfere with the proper enforcement of the R.R.K.B., he can be dethroned and the next in line to the throne is to immediately assume the responsibilities of the monarchy?" Kevin asked as he ducked out of the way of the King's, or rather the ex-King's hands.

"That's easy. Its number 42," the lawyer shouted as Kevin, closely followed by the ex-King, then the Princess, and then the congregation, all ran out of the tent. The congregation, though, did not stay out of the tent for more than half a heartbeat. A few brave ones poked their heads out of the opening and saw, for them, an awesome sight.

A huge, angry-looking dragon was standing right outside the tent, her large leathery wings slowly flapping, and smoke curling out of her nostrils. Below her chest, one shoulder resting against her left foreleg stood Kevin looking very relaxed. Archie was standing, as though he had been turned to stone, looking up at the behemoth. Princess Maybel ran over to Kevin and kissed him passionately.

PRINCE GASTON AND PRINCESS MAYBEL AT THE ALTAR.

When the shock of seeing Kevin and Millicent had worn off, the Princess asked the question that we all wanted to ask, but didn't have time for earlier when Kevin first appeared at the back of the tent.

"What happened? The last we saw of you was when you went back into Millicent's cave and there was a terrifying scream followed by a huge fireball?"

Kevin replied by telling how, when he re-entered the cave, Millicent pounced on him hoping to catch him off guard, as the tiny amount of Otter Oil he had used before had worn off. However, Millicent had made another mistake. She had been so excited about getting Kevin she could not keep still as she hid behind a rock. When Kevin heard her wings rustling he knew exactly what was happening, and this time jumped up on to the rock and stabbed Millicent with his sword. The wound though, was not very deep, and did not really hurt Millicent. It was, however, big enough for Kevin to pour the rest of the Otter Oil into the wound. It was then when Millicent had screamed in frustration. The huge fireball was spat out at the same time. Millicent was now bound to Kevin forever. In all honesty, Millicent was really quite happy as she now had a family. A rather strange family, even for a dragon, but nonetheless a family that cared about her.

Two weeks later, after new invitations were sent out and Prince Gaston had returned, Queen Maybel was escorted up the aisle of a freshly decorated tent, filled with a much happier and lighthearted crowd than before. Her brand new dress made of pure silk was even more stunning than the fake one was. It was most definitely Sue Inng's best work ever. The Chancellor stood sulking at the back of the tent, wearing a very plain brown suit. Grean-the-Grocer and Blough-the-Glassmaker were very proud to be the ushers and the small boy who had asked all those questions in Millicent's cave, was the ring bearer.

At the altar, Prince Gaston, dressed in the ceremonial uniform of the Prince of Arabacca, turned to watch the beautiful blushing bride, as she gracefully glided up the aisle towards him. His smile warmed her heart. Queen Maybel stopped at the last pew before the altar and bent to kiss her father's forehead. Archie looked up and smiled a warm smile at his beautiful daughter. Secretly King Archibald was very happy to be free of the pressures of running the kingdom. Maybel turned to her mother, who quickly stuffed a copy of her diet plan under her seat and blew Maybel a kiss. Maybel turned and stood next to Prince Gaston. They looked intently into each other's eyes for a while, and then turned to face the altar and the Bishop.

Prince Gaston was thinking he was the luckiest man in the world.

As best man at his best friend's wedding.

Kevin, who was standing next to the bishop, walked around the altar and took Maybel's hand as Prince Gaston stepped to one side. Kevin grinning a huge grin, stood with his bride-to-be facing the Bishop. As the ceremony progressed, Kevin and Maybel turned to each other, gazing with undying love into one another's eyes.

When the Bishop came to the impediment part of the ceremony, a nervous giggle rippled through the congregation. Soon it was time for Kevin and Maybel to say 'I do' and as they did, a joyful tear rolled down everyone's cheek. Even Millicent, who watched through a freshly made hole in the roof of the tent, shed a tear or two.

After all of the celebrations were over and all the guests had returned to their homes, Queen Maybel wondered why Kevin had gone back into Millicent's cave anyway. Kevin explained he was trying to find the treasure all dragons love to hoard. He suspected the real crown jewels of Blognasee were with the treasure, as many of the legends he had read seemed to indicate. However, after he had tamed Millicent for the second time, and asked her exactly where her treasure was, Millicent explained the treasure had been stolen while she was out picking her favorite food, many years before.

Kevin spent the next couple of days searching the cave, but found nothing. He decided to return to Spag-Bol and catch up with Maybel. By the time he got to Spag-Bol, they had all left and he was told the princess was going to get married the very next day to Prince Colah.

Upon hearing the news, Kevin made Millicent fly through the night to get to Lassaggnee before the ceremony. He was determined to marry the love of his life.

When Kevin, grinning, said "...but as I couldn't find her, I decided to marry you instead..." Queen Maybel jumped on him and they rolled around on the floor laughing, as though they had not a care in the world.

Naturally, everybody lived happily ever after, (sort of, but that's yet another story). Even Millicent, who, at first had a hard time convincing people that eating people was too revolting of an idea for her, was accepted by the people of Blognasee.

There are all sorts of advantages to having a large dragon around, one's enemies tend to get out of one's way and are more reluctant to bother one. Then there are all the tournaments, where brave knights from all over are keen to test themselves against a dragon. To win against a dragon the knight need only "stab" a dragon in any one of three vulnerable places. The rules were rather strict though, the "stabbing" was done with a lance that looked like a very large paintbrush that, hopefully, left a smear of paint on the dragon. The dragons could only warm the knights to the point of discomfort; imagine sitting in a tin can on the hottest day of the year. As soon as the knight had had enough, he could signal his resignation and that would end the match. Some knights tried to use the power of Dragon Roses, but the taste was so terrible most could not eat enough of them. Kevin on the other hand had grown rather fond of the unique flavor; a little like a mixture of raw onions and green tea ice cream with the texture of over cooked rice pudding. As Millicent and Kevin spent a good amount of time training -Kevin was getting very adept with various weapons- they soon became the biggest attraction at the tournaments and could command a higher than normal fee.

So with all of the money Kevin and Millicent were bringing in, the neighboring kingdoms no longer thought of the Blognassians as "their poor cousins."

And that is the story of how just plain Kevin Plane, became Kevin-the-Brave.

WHAT EVER HAPPENED TO...

For those of you who are wondering...

The frogs decided to escape to the sanctuary of the dark and not so scary forest and then they found a very nice very large damp cave to settle into. Prince Colah had also found a very nice very large damp cave. He was about to move out, because it was suddenly filled with the sound of hundreds of frogs croaking, when one of the frogs convinced him that if he stayed and kissed the right frog he would find the princess of his dreams. According to legend he is still deep in the heart of the cave trying to find the frog of his dreams, some say he has even begun to look like a frog.

The Chancellor was stripped of his position and fine clothing and was given the title of Fertilizer and Refuse Technician, whose job was to keep the streets clear of anything the horses, other large animals and Millicent left behind. He soon became known as Frank-the-Fart. It did not take him long though to work out he could start selling the ...fertilizer... to the local rose growers and soon he was earning enough money to payback all the money he had stolen from the kingdom.

The Captain-of-the-guard was pleasantly surprised to be reassigned to the royal kitchens as the head dishwasher. A job he knew very well and actually enjoyed.

The lieutenant was once again disappointed that he was not promoted to Captain-of-the-guard. Smiler LeCarry was given that job and soon had the Queen's Guard whipped into one of the most formidable troops in the known world. They were often called in to settle disputes between warring kingdoms. Most of the time they did not have to leave Blognasee, as soon as the combatants heard the Queen's Guard of Blognasee was going to "sort things out" the combatants stopped fighting and settled their differences peacefully. Of course having a rather large dragon at their disposal helped the Queen's Guard's reputation enormously.

All of the soldiers of Blognasee enjoyed receiving new uniforms that fit them perfectly and their pay was raised, so they spent more in the shops of Lassaggnee and the Big Bore Inn, which meant the villagers prospered too. Grean-the-grocer, Cirloin-the-Butcher and Bar-the-Bar, Kevin's dad, all had their signs repainted so their names or professions were spelled correctly.

The three footmen and other castle staff were also given new uniforms and better pay so they too started to take more pride in their work. So much so the three footmen, began a school to train others in the art of Footmanship and became very successful.

The Dastardly Pirate DeAmonté, who had left the pirating profession and was now offering, "Theme Cruises," was given the task of sailing to the Isle of Kiiddz and collecting any storytellers wanting to leave. He had to make six trips.

The School for Wayward Princes and Princesses was eventually closed and the building was turned into a college for the arts.

King Archibald and Queen Hortense enjoyed their retirement by travelling all over the known world visiting the other kings and queens and became great ambassadors for Queen Maybel and Prince Kevin.

Oh and the top of the Tall Tower was repaired so it would make the perfect home for about thirty-eight crows, who were very appreciative of their new home and whenever they saw something amiss in the world, they would fly down and let the Sergeant-of-the-crows know, he would then tell the lieutenant who would tell the Captain-of-the-Guard, who would tell the Sergeant-at-arms to dispatch the Queen's Guard.

THE END

Made in the USA
Monee, IL
02 June 2020